Barbary Slave

A NOVEL BY

PETER HOLLAND

Brigand

First published by Brigand in 2018
Second edition published by Brigand in 2019

Brigand Press,
All contact: info@brigand.london

Front cover design by
www.scottpearce.co.uk

A catalogue record for this book is
available from the British Library
Printed and Bound in Great Britain by CPI
Group (UK) Ltd, Croydon CR0 4YY

ISBN 978-1-912978-16-8

Author's Note

The idea for writing this book came from two sources.

The first was a wonderful short holiday in Istanbul four years ago. It left me thinking it must be the most historical city in the world. I accept others may disagree but I was overwhelmed standing in the Hagia Sophia, looking up in awe at the huge dome, built in the seventh century, almost 1,000 years before Wren's St Paul's Cathedral. What must it have been like for the doomed Byzantine Christians, who gathered there before the fall of Constantinople to the Ottomans in 1453? Every Christian within the city walls was put to the sword, or taken into slavery.

Two years after that trip I started my MA in Early Modern History at Birkbeck College, University of London. In the second term I had the good fortune to be able to choose a unit of study on Venice and Istanbul, looking at the importance of these two cities in the Mediterranean and beyond in the early modern period (1500-1800).

I became fascinated by this area of study, and in particular, a little known subject in British history, the 'white slave trade'. Having completed a 5,000 word essay on the subject, I could not help thinking there was a story to be told and began to plot it in my mind. Having talked to several friends and family members, I was encouraged by them to have a go at writing the story I enthusiastically told to them. One such friend, a university lecturer, accomplished academic and writer of several books, said it was a great subject for a novel but "don't write it until you've finished your MA." Others said "start writing it now, before you forget." I took the second option, a break from my MA dissertation, thinking about nothing else and writing the first draft in five months.

This novel is historical fiction, a story with a fictional plot and characters. The exception being Murat Reis, formerly Dutchman Jan Janszoon van Haarlem, who was very real, as captives, taken from Iceland in 1627 and Ireland in 1631, found to their cost. The raid on Baltimore, Ireland, in June 1631 is true, but the raid on Mevagissey a few days earlier as described in the book is fiction.

However, it is fair to say that all dates, events and numbers are as accurate as is possible. They are based on research and reading I did in 2017 for the unit of study described above. The texts I used are listed in the bibliography I have included at the back of the book, which I realise is unusual for a novel, but I feel it is justified for one which has rather a lot of historical data. For anyone who wants to read about the subject in more detail, and from far greater scholars than me, I recommend the work of Linda Colley, Robert Davis and Daniel Vitkus, all respected academics.

I would like to thank the following for their help, listening, reading and editing:

Jane Tiplady
Carole Harr
Philip Tew
Gavin Evans

Any surviving errors are my responsibilty.

Contents

Moriscos and Corsairs

Spain, January 1492. After 780 years of Muslim conquest and occupation, King Ferdinand and Queen Isabella end ten years of war against the Spanish Moors with the surrender of Granada. Spain would never again be ruled by the followers of Mohammed.

After victory, Christian Spain decided it would not tolerate other religions. In July 1492 all Jews, 200,000 of them, were forcibly expelled, two centuries after England's Edward I had done the same.

What to do about the Iberian Peninsula's Muslims was more difficult and complicated. The fighting at the end of the Reconquista saw the death or enslavement of 100,000 Moors in Castille. In that kingdom Isabella's rule saw 200,000 converted to Christianity, the former Spanish Muslims becoming Moriscos. Another 200,000 Muslims emigrated to safety in North Africa.

Ten years later Isabella made conversion compulsory for all Moors in Castille and in 1526 Charles V did the same in Aragon. Muslim conversos were known as Moriscos but their safety was not secure and they faced deep suspicion. Many Jewish and Muslim converts to Christianity were believed to be secretly practising their old religions and they always faced suspicion from the Spanish Inquisition.

By 1568 Moriscos in the former Muslim stronghold of Granada rebelled and it took three years to crush them. Initially the defeated Moriscos were simply displaced and moved to other parts of Spain. However eventually their fate was the same as that of the Jews and in 1609 all 300,000 Moriscos were expelled from Spain.

So, after co-existing for eight centuries and another 100 plus years of forced conversions, suspicion, intolerance and rebellion, Spain was finally rid of all non-Catholic Christians. Spain was becoming the wealthiest and one of the most powerful nations in Europe, largely financed by the success of its empire across the Atlantic.

But there was a consequence and legacy to the expulsion of non-Christians. Just across the Straits of Gibraltar, along the coast of North Africa, the descendants of the Muslims and Moriscos who had fled or were expelled, settled in the small city states and kingdoms that are today known as Morocco, Tunisia and Algeria. What should they do, other than farm, fish and trade. What could they trade and could they forgive or forget?

Moriscos joined the Barbary communities along the North African coastline, named after the Berbers. There they found a society based on one dominant economic activity: Slavery. All along that Barbary coastline were men who had become expert in raiding the Mediterranean, European Atlantic coastline and shipping routes. Highly organised pirates called Corsairs, they took what they could from coastal communities and ships, their most prized targets being men and women.

Over a period of three hundred years from 1500 to 1800 Barbary Corsairs seized over 1,000,000 European captives and whilst some never left the Barbary coast towns and cities, the men used for hard labour and a smaller number of women as concubines, the overwhelming majority were sold into a growing empire to the East with an insatiable appetite for slaves, the Ottoman Empire.

Scholars estimate that in the 17th century when the empire was at its height, it had an average of 300,000 slaves in chains in any given year. There were 100,000 slaves in in the great city of Istanbul in 1609. Mortality rates were high, particularly amongst those slaves whose fate it was to be a galley slave. These slaves were not 'bred' as they were in the Americas, resulting in a constant demand to replace those who died.

With the expulsion of the Moriscos from Spain, the ranks of Barbary Corsairs swelled with men who were hungry for wealth and revenge. Other events added to the anger and zeal of the slave-seeking pirates, which would make the fate of vulnerable European Christians even more precarious. In 1607 an attack on the Algerian town of Bona, resulting in the burning of the town, the killing of over 470 and more than 1,400 Muslims being taken into slavery. Barbary states were enraged and their response affected European coastal communities and shipping for decades to come.

In 1604 England's new King James I, who had come down from Scotland to succeed his cousin Elizabeth, decided to end decades of war with Spain by signing a treaty that aligned England with the most powerful Catholic state in Europe. As it was primarily Spain and the Italian states that provided the most opposition to Ottoman expansion in the Mediterranean, England was placed in a position at odds with Ottoman ambitions, thereby becoming fair game for Barbary Corsairs.

Those following decades were dramatic and costly. James' predecessor, Elizabeth, had signed treaties and traded with Barbary States, a shrewd political move that largely secured safe passage for English ships and supported rogue states that were a thorn in the side of Spain, England's greatest enemy during her reign. However following James's treaty, by 1616 Algiers alone had seized over 450 English shipping vessels, and this was just the beginning. Between 1610 and 1640 Cornwall and Devon lost a fifth of their shipping to Barbary Corsairs. 1625 was a particularly bad year, in which almost a thousand sailors and fishermen from the West Country port of Plymouth were seized and taken into slavery, most of them from within 30 miles of shore.

That first half of the 17th century was the nadir for the British Isles in terms of attacks from Barbary Corsairs. Between 1600 and the early 1640s Corsairs seized more than 800 English, Scottish, Welsh and Irish vessels, taking their cargo and placing their crews and passengers into captivity, which invariably meant the rest of their lives in bondage. Thousands of men and women from the British Isles were enslaved in this 40-year period. A relatively small number compared to other European states, particularly those with coastlines along the Mediterranean, but still significant for the government and even more so for the fishing and trading communities in the coastal towns and villages.

Charles I inherited a problem that made his difficult reign even more uncomfortable. In 1625 Barbary Corsairs in some 30 ships were sighted off the coast of St Ives in Cornwall. Six years later in 1631 was a notorious raid on the small fishing town of Baltimore in the south-west corner of Ireland, subsequently known as the Sack of Baltimore. A large Barbary force led by Dutchman Jan Janszoon, famously known as Murat Reis, seized over 120 men, women and children, who were taken back to the slave markets of Algiers and Salle.

Said

"Said, Said! Come, we must go now."

His mother Aisha looked worried, Fatima his grandmother was wailing. The day had finally come, they were leaving their home. Well it had been their home since before he was born but it wasn't their ancestral home, it wasn't the soil his family and forefathers had lived on for over 700 years. That land was along the coastline of Granada, where his family had supported their families through fishing, farming, different trades and commerce. It had been a good life. His family and whole village had been forced to move inland following rebellions when his father was a young boy. Said had grown up as a small boy listening to his parents, grandparents, uncles, cousins talking about the old days. This village and land that he'd known as home was inland, away from the coast. Less fertile land, no fishing in the sea, just a few rivers and streams that were dry for much of the summer.

He could remember the comments he'd heard a hundred times:

"Once we were proud Muslims, Spanish Muslims who built the beautiful Alhambra."

"Look at what we've become, conversos, to stay alive we've been forced to become infidels, Moriscos worshipping in churches."

"Our children have been born into Christianity, our sons have never entered a mosque."

"We have been denied the religion of our fathers, unable to follow the teachings of the prophet."

Said had not known any different, a boy of just nine years. It didn't really matter to him, he'd been happy and felt safe, well he did until now in the year 1609. Now they must all leave as soon as they could, taking only what they could carry.

"Quickly Said, the soldiers will be here soon, we must go now, or face enslavement or death."

His mother was repeating the rumours that had reached them from other villages. They'd heard of the Inquisition and how Morisco men had been taken, questioned, tortured and executed, some even burned alive. The King was sending yet more soldiers to push the once proud Spanish Muslims, now despised Morisco converts, towards the sea. Said couldn't know how many of his people were being forced to leave, he'd heard his father say to his uncle that it was a countless number of men, women and children.

"We will go across the sea to Morocco," his father said. Said had never seen the sea, which made him both nervous and excited.

"Your grandfather was once a fisherman, as well as a farmer. You can learn to swim and you will love the feeling of the cool sea wind."

His father, Ahmed, wanted to allay the fears he knew his son must be feeling, particularly being exposed so much to the wailing and crying of his grandmother. It was true, having been born deep inland in Granada away from the sea, he had only ever known searing hot summers, watching his family struggle to grow food to feed themselves, farming dry barren soil.

And so finally the day had arrived and they, along with twenty other families from their village, headed south walking towards the coast. Ahmed reckoned on it taking three to four days but that would be a challenge as they carried their belongings. Only Fatima was free of the burden of carrying possessions. However this was still a journey that would be difficult for a frail woman, who in her seventy-fourth year had not walked any distance for longer than Said had been alive.

Fatima's physical and mental strength had seemed to decline in the weeks since they had learnt of the expulsion order. The weeping and wailing Said had been listening to for days was her departure lament, not just from their home but from life as well. She had never been back to the village by the coast where she'd grown as a girl and young woman. She had not been alive when the Christians finally completed what they called the Reconquista, before which time Muslims ruled Granada. Her grandmother had lived in that time and told Fatima of what it was like under Muslim rule, following the teachings of the prophet.

After two days marching in the summer heat and struggling to find water in dried up rivers, Fatima stopped and lay down.

"Come mother" Ahmed urged. "We cannot dwell here; the soldiers are not far behind and will kill anyone who doesn't make it to the sea."

Fatima did not care and lay herself down under an olive tree, she didn't even speak, just closed her eyes and stopped breathing. Said had never seen someone die in front of him with his own eyes, it seemed to be a peaceful end and he wondered if death was always like that. Burying Fatima was not easy, the summer sun had dried the soil so it was almost as hard as the rocks that littered that inland area of Granada. Ahmed and two neighbours laboured for two hours, as their families rested, shading themselves from the sun. Eventually she was laid to rest in a shallow grave, care being taken to leave no markings or trace that might indicate she was a Morisco, a former Muslim, for fear of her grave being dug up and desecrated.

"She hasn't been welcome here since she was born, but she couldn't bear to leave."

Ahmed was sad for the loss of his mother but thought it was better for her to leave the world now, rather than endure the ordeal of moving across the sea, even if it was to a land they had heard was friendly towards his people. Maybe she could even have visited a Mosque just one more time. But it was not to be and having taken time to bury his mother, his thoughts and efforts were to get his family to the coast as quickly as possible and across the sea to Morocco, Algiers or Tunis.

Two days after the death of Fatima, Said and his family along with ninety-five others from his village, reached the once great fortified coastal town of Almeria. For 500 years it had been a Muslim stronghold. Its rulers had provided security and it grew rich through trade, particularly with the buying and selling of beautiful silk fabrics. However, after many sieges it finally fell to the Christian Reconquista in 1489, one of the last great Muslim strongholds in Spain to fall to the infidel. Said had heard his father, grandfather and uncles talk about how the Christians rejoiced over its capture, but that their joy didn't last long, as Allah destroyed much of the town and its fortifications through an earthquake thirty-three years later, leaving a shell of what it had once been.

Ahmed would've liked to bring his son to this once great Muslim town in happier circumstances, where he could've seen where great mosques once stood. As they entered the town they became aware of other Moriscos making the same journey from other parts of Granada and the Almeria region, but they could not have anticipated the scene that met them inside the town, particularly down at the portside.

Said had never seen a boat or ship before, yet before him sat more than he could count. Small fishing boats, larger cargo boats and two huge galleys. They were all packed into the town's quay, manned by men of different appearances, both physically and in dress. Each vessel seemed to be dominated by one man, who was to be heard shouting commands to members of his crew, although most were not using the Spanish language or dialect of Granada that Said was familiar with. Ahmed looked in amazement and realised the enormity of the movement of people, of which he and his family were a tiny part.

Thousands of people, too many to count, seeking a passage across the sea, away from Spain forever. Families from all over southern Spain had left their homes and made their way to this port. Despite their numbers there was great fear of what could happen to them trapped inside the walls of the town. Stories of slaughter by Christian Crusaders was part of Muslim history and had been kept alive in Morisco communities even after the forced conversos of the last hundred years.

"Never forget the slaughter of 1099."

Said had heard this from his elders many times.

"Crusading Christian infidels killed every Muslim, every Jew, every man, woman and child inside the gates of Jerusalem. All 70,000 of them."

There were soldiers but they were keeping their distance from the thousands of families gathering at the port to migrate. Optimists amongst the Moriscos said this was to safeguard their departure from Spanish soil, as was promised by the Grand Council. It was true that the fear of marauding gangs of Christians who might steal, rape and kill had not materialised on the four days walk to the coast. However, pessimists feared this was just part of a plan by the government to gather all Moriscos at several key ports, then set about their complete annihilation by the Spanish army.

"We would be trapped and would face the same fate of our Muslim brothers in Jerusalem in 1099 and so many others in sieges across different lands since those days. The Christians always turn to the same brutal methods in the end."

These two conflicting views had filled the Moriscos with a dreadful fear of the unknown but they had no real choice. If they'd stayed in their villages they faced death, so here Ahmed's family were and would be, hopefully for as short a time as possible, until he could secure their passage.

The whole town and particularly the port found itself in total chaos. The population of Almeria had been largely Moriscos, as it had always been an important point of defence for Muslim Spain. For over a century the governance of the town had been in the hands of the Spanish Christian conquerors, along with the large land owners, ownership of the textiles traders, and town council leaders. The former Spanish Moors who were forced to convert were second-class citizens, that is if they were important enough in terms of skills to save them from being driven out of the town to a barren piece of land like Said's family fifty years earlier.

With news of the expulsion of all Moriscos from Spain, Almeria like a number of ports along the south coast was invaded by enterprising traders who saw an opportunity. 300,000 Moriscos needed safe passage and very few had boats. In the scramble that ensued boat and ship owners and merchants from all of Spain's coastal towns, as well as from across the sea, converged on these ports, smelling the chance to get rich quick.

Said stood open-mouthed at the sight before him. Hundreds of ships, a mass of humanity and the commercial chaos of a town and port that had become one big market place selling the same product. For the first but not last time in his life he saw something he'd never seen before, something none of his family had seen, not even the recently buried Fatima: A handful of men of completely different appearance, both physically in their features and also in their dress. Only after some time did he and Ahmed learn that they were Jews, a people who had been expelled from Spain by the Christians, famous for their skill in commerce. It would seem the Spanish had allowed some of these people, who they despised, to return to help in the process of expelling the Moriscos. Muslim sailors and merchants were also allowed into the port with their ships to complete the expulsion. It seemed to Said there must be thousands of Moriscos gathering in Almeria, all seeking safe passage to North Africa.

"Where shall we go to in Africa father?" Said asked. Ahmed had been thinking about this during the four-day march from their village to the coast. In fact, he'd been thinking about it for months, possibly years. Ahmed was not alone, all of the family leaders who made the march had it on their minds and talked about it furtively, away from their wives and children for fear of scaring them. Getting to the coast was one thing but then securing passage and a safe destination was another matter. They knew that at sea they were no longer in control of their fate, at the mercy of seamen and merchants, who were little more than pirates.

"What's to stop them from taking our money for the passage, taking us out to sea, killing us and returning to repeat the same thing over and over?"

"These men are pirates and want only gold and silver."

"Well at least they won't sell us into slavery, Barbary sailors only enslave Christians…"

"Don't be so sure, they wouldn't sell us to the Ottomans but what's to stop them from sailing to Italy and selling us to the Genoese or Venetians?"

These were the conversations and thoughts of the family leaders who had to decide. But they had no choice, they must leave Spain and they had to trust the Jews, who acted as agents, Barbary merchants and seamen.

"We will go to Algiers my son." Ahmed replied to Said's question. He spoke calmly and with kindness, as he had always done to his nine-year old son, his beautiful boy, despite the worry and anxiety he felt, not knowing quite what they would be heading to.

"Father, other boys say Morocco is very close, just one day of sailing. Why don't we go there, I'm afraid of storms at sea. A boy said the ships can sink and everyone drowns. Father, can you swim, I can't, would you save me?"

Ahmed looked at him, "don't worry Said, I will always take care of you." Words like these were uttered by thousands of Morisco fathers trying to get their families to safety, all of them knowing it was a promise they couldn't guarantee.

"We're going to Algiers Said."

"But that is farther away."

"Yes, but only five days in the ship and it is a safer place for us."

"Why is it safer father?"

His son was intelligent and would perpetually ask why, always wanting to understand, always wanting to learn, to gain wisdom. Ahmed was conscious of Said's nervousness so he took the opportunity to entertain his son with another history story, which he knew he enjoyed. It helped to pass the time and reassured the young boy.

"Morocco is ruled by a great man but it is not as safe because Algiers, is part of the Ottoman Empire. It rules itself but is protected by the Sultan in Istanbul. This has been the way for eighty years since the days of the greatest of all Sultans Suleiman the Magnificent."

Said loved to listen to his father tell stories of the past and Islam's victories over the Christians.

"Even the Holy Roman Emperor Charles, the most powerful man in Christendom, tried to capture Algiers and failed. He lost a great armada and 30,000 men."

Said's eyes were wide open, he was entranced at the thought of a Christian army of 30,000 being killed or taken into slavery by Muslims.

"Algiers is where we will go, it's where we will be safe my son."

Ahmed put his arm around Said's shoulders, gave him a hug and his son looked happier.

Thankfully the voyage was calm and without problems. Said's first experience of the sea, he wasn't to know that it would be the first of many voyages, that he would become an expert sailor, skilled fighter and more. Right there in the summer of 1609 as a nine-year old boy he felt happy, relieved that his family had at last got away from Spain and was heading for the security of Algiers and the protection Ahmed, the great Sultan of Istanbul. He liked the coincidence that his father had the same name. Anyway, he had never felt comfortable and welcome in Spain, his people had been forced to convert from Islam to Christianity but surreptitiously stayed true to Mohammed.

The boat on which they were able to secure their crossing was formerly a cargo vessel, manned by a captain and four crew, it accommodated twelve families that numbered some sixty Moriscos, ranging in age from a three months-old infant to several elders in their eighth decade. There was not a lot of spare space, the captain had no intention of not maximising his revenue from making the voyage to Africa. However, the passengers felt comfortable as they could lay down to sleep and tarpaulins offered shade from the sun.

Said could sense the optimism shared by his family and the other passengers. The sea air and wind on his face made him feel free, perhaps he could become a sailor he thought to himself, it seemed to be a good life. He wasn't to know that it was an ambition he would go on to achieve.

Having sailed south out of Almeria, they turned towards the East as they sailed close to the African coastline, offering them protection from possible Christian pirates and warships. Barbary shipping was fair game for any Christians. For Said and the other young Morisco boys it was exciting to see the land of the continent that would be their new home.

"It was hot in summer where we lived. I've been told Africa is even hotter, and there's the Great Desert."

"Yes, but my brother told me all the great cities and towns are by the sea, so we can swim everyday."

Said listened to the other boys and thought carefully about what lay ahead for him and his family, 'I think it will be better; Algiers, Africa, the protection of the Sultan, no more threats from Christians.' He kept looking east and south, towards places that offered his family and all Moriscos a better life than the one they left behind in Spain.

Then on the fifth day the ship altered course, turned south around a large headland and there in a large bay was a heavily fortified city.

"Algiers, Algiers!"

The cry went up and Said rushed to the starboard side of the ship to see. Everyone was cheering and happy, the fears of the elders were proving to be unfounded, there had been no shackles, the crew had been friendly calling the Moriscos their Muslim brothers. And now they sailed into the large bay, moving smoothly towards the port. Algiers Bay provided a large natural harbour and was crammed with boats of all sizes, just like Almeria. However, it was more heavily fortified, with a great wall circling the city. Behind the city and to the sides the land rose steeply to clifftops. It was an imposing sight and the quayside was packed with humanity, most of which seemed to be attached to one of the vessels.

To confirm there had been no reason for their fears, the family leaders were relieved to find that disembarkation for their families was carried out with help and kindness from fierce looking soldiers who served the Pasha of Algiers. He ruled the city and surrounding territory and was answerable to only one man, the great Sultan in Istanbul, who ruled over millions throughout the Ottoman Empire.

Khaled

After the anxiety of getting to the Spanish coast, making the voyage across the Mediterranean and sailing along the North African coastline, life for Said's family began to feel more secure. Ahmed found a small home for them just outside the city wall, where it seemed new buildings appeared almost every day. It would be a while before Said realised why this great city was able to grow so quickly, adding people and buildings like plants overnight.

"The men who work seem never to rest father."

"Yes, they work very hard."

Ahmed did not feel inclined to explain to his nine-year-old son what a life in bondage would mean for those poor souls, whether they were Christian or any other religion. Said had not seen slaves before and he would learn about them in good time.

Ahmed didn't need to worry; his son was an intelligent boy and quickly learnt how the world worked by exploring the city with his friends. Said knew he must be polite and respectful, learn Arabic the language of Algiers and the language of the Koran. He went to the mosque daily and learned to pray five times a day. The Iman organised a school and even fed the boys, encouraging them to embrace Islam. Here Said and other recent arrivals learnt Arabic and Islamic history with more accurate accounts of the great Ottoman Sultans, like Suleiman the Magnificent from the previous century, the fall of Constantinople in 1453, and before that Salahdin's capture of Jerusalem. All of this was seen by the Pasha as important in making the great influx of Moriscos feel proud of their Islamic heritage, confident that Algiers would be their home, thereby making them loyal to him and the Sultan in Istanbul.

Along with the freedom they had never known in Spain, the opportunity Said and his friends enjoyed most was to wander the busy streets and alleys of this chaotic and busy city. Said learned to swim, every boy in Algiers could swim and when they got too hot they could always bathe, diving into the sea from the rocks to the sides of the harbour.

He had never seen anyone different from his Morisco community and sometimes fairer skinned Spaniards from the north. However, Algiers was a throng of humanity with people of every complexion, brown like himself, slightly darker Berbers, black Africans and various shades of white people. Arabic was the primary language but he would also hear numerous other tongues, which he did not understand. Observing the people with the wide range of complexions, Said also began to understand the social structure of Algiers, complicated by different religions, races and nationalities.

Muslims were at the top, and whilst as believers in the Prophet and Allah they were all equal, in terms of political and economic power, the Berbers were most senior, along with visiting Ottoman officials, seamen and soldiers, who were always treated as honoured guests. All Muslims were free men, which included many black Africans. However, there were also black Africans who were slaves, which confused Said.

" Why are some of the Africans free men, whilst some of them are slaves, father?"

“If an African is a Muslim he is a free man, just like all other Muslims, but if he is not he is likely to be a slave, my son.”

Said learnt that Algiers was built on the misery of captives brought there from all directions, over land and by sea. Most seemed to be either white Europeans, or black Africans. The white slaves were brought in on ships but the Africans often came over land from the south, across the Great Desert. Jews seemed to enjoy a liberty they were not guaranteed living amongst Christians in Europe. There were fewer of them than any other group but they were very distinctive in their way of dressing and their appearance. Only the men were seen in public and they were usually mature in age, merchants, money lenders and notaries of law. Their hair was well-kept and long, as were their beards. They wore long robes that hid their physical frame, along with their pockets and small bags, that might contain coins, gold or silver. Muslims did not socialise with them but there was a mutual respect and Said got the impression Jews were important in the complicated world of trade. They seemed to be able to arrange for almost anything to be brought to Algiers, or to be delivered to another port around the Mediterranean and beyond.

The Jews seemed to be less involved with the slaves at the bottom of Algiers social structure. Almost every Christian in Algiers was a slave, although there was a small number who were not. Said was shocked to see the masses of largely white Christian slaves. They were most obvious down in the port area in the slave market, where they were bought and sold, often being loaded onto ships for immediate transport to their new masters.

Said noticed that few of the Christian slaves were old.

"Father, do the old ones die on the journey?" He asked the question after some months of exploring the town and observing the workings of the thriving slave market.

"No Said, when they take captives the Corsairs are not interested in old men and women."

"Why not father, older men can do things and have knowledge and wisdom. And old women can clean, cook and help women in childbirth."

"They need to be fit and strong Said."

"But why are there so many more men than women father?"

Ahmed did not want to get into a conversation with Said about the fate of the young women in the slave markets so tried to offer as reasonable a reply as possible,

"I'm not a Corsair slaver Said; maybe it's because men are stronger than women."

This would have to do, Ahmed knew Said would find out for himself eventually. Said could tell his father was getting somewhat irritated by these questions and accepted this explanation.

If the Christian slaves were not in the market being bought and sold, they could sometimes be seen at different places in the town doing back-breaking work. Algiers was constantly being fortified and expanded, which involved the work of hundreds of men working throughout the day in the searing heat. They were closely guarded by fierce looking Berbers and punishment for not working hard was brutal and swift. Said winced and turned away the first time he saw a man in chains being whipped. The guards would stop short of killing slaves, Said later realised they were not worth anything dead, but examples would be made to motivate the other slaves to work hard. He was fascinated by slavery and how the process worked, what it was to be enslaved. But it would be some years before he fully understood that it was all about money and power.

The slaves were never seen at night. They were returned to Bagnos, large secured buildings, where they were kept under lock and key. Slaves could be severely punished for being outside after sunset.

"Could they escape if they got out of the Bagnos father?"

"Where would they go Said? To the north is the sea and to the south is the Great Desert."

It was a shock for Said to see the way the slaves were treated, having never witnessed such brutality by one man to another. He had been aware of stories of mistreatment of his own people by the Christians back in Spain, but being only nine years old and living in a village remote from aggressive Christians, he had never seen the cruelty of which people were capable. Severe beatings were common, although rarely resulting in death, at least not there when the beatings occurred. He learnt that sometimes the beatings were so severe the slaves might get ill and die as a result of their wounds.

"That one was too weak anyway." Slave guards would simply say.

Said asked the older boys why the Christian slaves were treated so severely. He found they were willing to be more open with him and questions he asked, unlike his father who seemed to being trying to protect him.

"Don't feel so sorry for them," Khaled said.

"Why?" Said asked.

"They, or their Christian brothers, attacked the town of Bona two years ago and showed no mercy. They killed nearly 500 of our brothers and sisters and took almost 1,500 back to Europe as slaves."

Said's eyes widened at the thought of the attack and he remembered his father saying they would be safe in Algiers. Could father be wrong, he asked himself.

"What do you think happened to those captives, do you think they're sitting under olive trees sipping tea?" Khaled asked his rhetorical question with a sneer.

Many times toward the end of his childhood, before entering adolescence, Said was left to his thoughts as he absorbed all the sounds and sights of the bustling city. One thing was for certain, he was happy to be in this wonderful, bustling place. He didn't miss the boring little village in Spain, which had formerly been his home. 'Would I have ever seen a Jew or African if we'd stayed there', he wondered to himself, 'never mind a slave'. His family were happier too, no longer told what to do and who to worship by the Spanish King and Bishops. Life under the rule of the great Sultan in Istanbul seemed to be more secure. The colours of Algiers were stark, with bright blue sea and sky, white and soft brown buildings, orange sand stretching around the edge of the bay. But it was the different shades and conditions of humanity that most interested him, leaving him to think 'I will stay here, make it my home, study, learn about the world and how it works'.

When the sun went down Said and his friends would sit on a wall and watch the slaves trudge wearily back to their Bagnos. Khaled and some of the boys would laugh and jeer at the pitiful line of men shackled together. Cruel jibes about the wives, daughters and sisters of the slave men didn't seem to draw any reaction from them, even though those who had been in Algiers for any time would understand some Arabic. The boys would even hurl the insults in Spanish or Italian if they thought it would be more effective. Said realised these men were now his enemy and they or their countrymen had done terrible things to Muslims like him and his family. But he couldn't bring himself to join the other boys in tormenting the slaves, their lives were miserable enough. He looked into the faces of the men as they walked past and couldn't stop himself from empathising with them. Perhaps he would change with time and become harder like Khaled. Even at this young age Said was more interested in slavery commercially, thinking about how much each captive might sell for, and why one might be worth more than another.

He learnt more and more about how slave trading worked. Brave Barbary Corsairs would take to sea, sometimes for months. They would follow the routes Christian trading ships sailed, looking for easy prey. Merchants and sailors rarely wanted to engage Barbary Corsairs in a fight, such was their fierce and ruthless reputation. Said felt a pride when he thought about this, 'Corsairs must be great men'. Christian ships would try to outrun them to safety but once they were caught they usually surrendered without a blow being landed. The sailors knew their fate and it was something they feared and lived with whenever they set sail from their home ports. Once captured some would ask to be allowed to convert to Islam, which could gain them their freedom, but the Corsairs would only allow them to ask for this once they were in Algiers, Salle or whichever Barbary town they were taken to in chains.

Said and the other boys witnessed the occasionally distraught but usually simply resigned captives disembarking in the port and being gathered in small pens like sheep. They did not receive the help and kindness Said's family had experienced, they were moved along with the help of whips and clubs. The only exceptions were the relatively small numbers of women, who were treated with firmness but less brutality. With age Said learned what his father had been reluctant to talk about when he first arrived at the age of nine. Some of the young women and girls were destined for a life working as domestic servants. If they were lucky the mistress of the house would be a kind woman. However, Said came to learn that most of the young woman and girls faced a future as a concubine; a sex slave for a master in Algiers, Istanbul or any one of a hundred Ottoman towns.

After a couple of years, as Said became an adolescent he could see for himself that some women were more pleasing to a man's eye than others. Seeing how the men and his friends looked at and talked about the young women and girls, he was glad he didn't have a sister. But there was no question that these beautiful creatures, so fair in complexion, drew emotions from him that he'd never experienced before.

The more beautiful slave girls were treated with great care. Said came to understand that Algiers was the major port and slave market along the Barbary coast and that the girls and young women were highly prized if they were considered beautiful. Most would be heading East towards Istanbul, where there were up to 100,000 slaves, albeit mainly men. He'd hear the slave traders call-out many times each week.

"Look at this beautiful, fair skinned maid, she could be bound for the Sultan's harem. One of you could have her as your own!"

For some of the men watching the sight of these young women was too much and they would be overcome with passion, although they were usually the ordinary Berbers who could not afford her, just as they might look longingly at a prized horse they knew they could never afford. The men who could afford the most beautiful girls were always calmer, more guarded and circumspect. Negotiating a price was a deal they'd struck many times before. They were dressed in the clothes of wealthy traders, powerful men in the service of a pasha or maybe the Sultan. Sometimes they were bidding for themselves, for their own pleasure and Said came to think he could identify these men as they showed some emotion at the conclusion of the deal, when they knew they would be enjoying the beautiful maid that very evening.

Khaled was two years older than Said and he would stare intently at the beautiful girls brought from the north and was more excited than his younger friend.

"Look at this one Said, her skin is like ivory, her hair is the colour of gold and her eyes are as blue as the sea."

Said would look and yes he could see the young maid was beautiful, but as a boy of 14 he wasn't as gripped by the sight of these mysterious girls as sixteen-year-old Khaled.

"One day I will have a maid like that for my own, she will be my concubine who will keep me warm at night."

"Would you make her your wife Khaled, or just a girl for your pleasure."

"If she converted to Islam, maybe I would make her my wife. You know the greatest of all Sultans, Suleiman the Magnificent, had many girls in his harem from the north, and one of them became his favourite and he made her his wife."

Said loved to listened to his slightly older, more worldly-wise friend.

"What was her name Khaled?"

"She was called Roxelana, Said. But she became known as Hurrem Sultan and was trusted by Suleiman above everyone else, even the Grand Viziers and Pashas who served him. She even advised and helped him run the empire, particularly when he was away conquering much of Europe."

"How do you know all this Khaled, you weren't there."
Said replied with a cheeky grin. Khaled gave a fixed stare, which could've been accompanied by a blow to another boy who questioned his integrity, but not Said, who Khaled was coming to love like a younger brother.

"Listen to you, little Morisco, you question everything."

Instead of a blow Khaled gave a sharp shoulder barge sending Said tumbling.

"Be careful you don't let any Ottomans hear you question the stories they tell about Suleiman and Roxelana."

He gave Said an affectionate grin, which turned to loud laughter. As Said stood up his left leg covered in a brown coat of what had to be either camel or horse shit.

"Argh, Khaled look at me, I will kill you…"

A chase followed and ended as they both got beyond the harbour and dived into the sea. After a swim, mutual ducking and a lot of laughter the two boys made their way home, still laughing together. Even through such small shared experiences they were developing a close friendship that would last for life.

As his teenage years progressed what really interested Said was how the Corsairs captured the slaves and the different types of ships that were used to chase down merchant ships, raid coastal towns and even fight battles. It was when he was about fifteen years of age that he decided he wanted to go to sea. He realised the Corsairs would not use the same size of ship for capturing a small trading vessel with only six men aboard, as they might to raid a town, fight a battle and capture a hundred or more slaves. Some of these ships were small and fast, used to chase their prey and over-run the crew, which was usually straightforward without opposition. Then the much larger ship would come alongside and the crew and cargo would be loaded. If a captured ship was thought worth keeping, perhaps it could fetch a price in the market, it would be sailed back to Algiers with a small crew, as the Corsairs then pressed on in search of greater prizes. If the captured ship was thought to be of no use it was sunk, leaving no trace of the vessel, cargo or crew. Just as he was fascinated by the commercial aspect of the slave market, Said thought a great deal about the different ships, their cost, size of crew and how many slaves they could carry.

Large Corsair galleys were truly a sight to behold and Said would stand in awe as they moved slowly into the bay and glide into Algiers' harbour. They were huge and his friends would say they could carry 1,000 men. He studied them from afar as often as he could, identifying each one by its colours and flags, many being not Corsairs but Ottoman warships. They were all galleys with long lines of oars as well as two great mainsails. The oars were twenty metres in length and there were up to twenty-five on each side of the ship. Each oar would be powered by five slaves, making a total of 250 slaves per large galley. People would talk of even larger Ottoman galleys powered by 500 slaves but Said didn't see those in Algiers. 'They must be kept at Istanbul ready to fight great naval battles for the Sultan' he thought to himself.

If Said had felt sympathy for the Christian slaves who faced daily hard labour in the town, he could not believe how severe life was for the galley slaves. He'd heard people say that once a captive was sold as a galley slave they might never set foot on land again in this life, which was often short. Shackled to a bench and the oar they worked alongside four other men. If they didn't row and keep in time they faced the whip. If they collapsed with fatigue or illness they were disposed of overboard. They didn't row if the ship was stationary, or if there was a storm and the captain didn't want the oars to be damaged. If the ship was fired on by cannon they could not escape. If the ship sank they drowned chained to their bench and oar.

"These men are no more than oxen that pull the plough."

Even Khaled expressed some sympathy for the poor souls doomed to a life chained to bench and oar.

"But Khaled the ox is not attached to its plough for every minute of its life, it can lay down at night."

Khaled just nodded in agreement as they both watched the galley from the rocks to the side of the harbour.

As well as the galley slaves on these large ships there would be the crew of ten to twenty men who were fierce fighters. These were the true Corsairs, men who sail the seas and fight any enemy. Also, the biggest ships were large enough to carry up to 100 soldiers and there was still space for captives and cargo they seized. Said loved the sight of these great vessels, manned by men he admired for their toughness and fearlessness. As a teenager he was prepared to compromise any reservations of the rights and wrongs of slavery. Yes, he had some sympathy for the men who were condemned to a life of hard labour on land and even worse at sea. But the likes of Khaled began to wear down any qualms and conscience, it was the way the world worked and the Christians were doing the same by enslaving Muslims. By the time he was 15 years of age, Said knew this was the life he wanted to pursue, he saw the Corsairs return to Algiers, welcomed as heroes and much richer than when they left.

Khaled shared Said's fascination and the two boys, only two years apart in age, spent much of their time watching the ships leave and return, usually full with valuable cargo, both human and non-human. Their shared ambition resulted in them becoming best friends, virtually brothers, whose parents saw as inseparable. When there were no ships in view that they could study together, they would talk and plan how they would become Corsairs. Many young Corsairs were the sons of Corsairs but because of losses in battle and storms, captains of ships would take young men to sea and raiding as apprentices. This was the route Khaled and Said would take, but they had to prove themselves as seamen who could sail a ship, as well as fighting soldiers.

"Khaled, we must learn to sail a ship, we must be experts."

"Yes Said, but we must also learn to fight, not like when we fight the other boys in the street. I mean we must learn to fight like soldiers, with sabres and daggers."

Said nodded, but at the age of fifteen, compared to Khaled's seventeen, he felt more comfortable with the thought of sailing a ship, than fighting another man with weapons.

"Could you kill a man, Khaled?"

Khaled just stared ahead across the Bay of Algiers and replied.

"Of course I can, and I will."

Said felt a cold chill as he looked at his older friend, his big brother, thinking 'please don't die Khaled'.

To set about achieving their ambition, Khaled and Said asked if they could help an old fisherman take his boat out, catch the fish, but most importantly learn how to sail. Mobasher had lost his own son in an accident, a fishing trip he told his son not to attempt. The weather looked to be getting rough but his son was obstinate and, like so many young men, thought he might be immortal. After his drowning, Mobasher felt like his world had collapsed but he still had a wife and three daughters to feed, so he had to carry-on fishing.

"Why did Allah decide I should have one son and three daughters. Why not three sons and one daughter?"

These were words Mobasher uttered a hundred times before Khaled and Said met him, and they were words they heard him say a thousand times in the two years they worked with him.

Mobasher agreed to take the two boys on as if it was a great sacrifice, when in reality it was very much in his interest. He knew he couldn't handle the boat and catch the fish by himself. He could lose the boat and the only means he had to feed his wife and daughters. Khaled and Said quickly realised this but after surviving the first weeks of the old man cursing and telling them "You will never make it as fishermen, never Corsairs!" they began to warm to him, and he to them. Mobasher's fishing boat was modest in size but comfortably accommodated three to five men and the carefully folded nets. The three of them found their natural positions, with Mobasher at the back controlling the rudder, perfectly placed to supervise two young willing students. Once instructed and shown, Said and Khaled learnt quickly and enthusiastically. It had been months since his own son had died and they were much younger, but they reminded him of his own beloved Nouredine when he was a teenage boy. Reliable and eager to learn, smiling and laughing, they worked hard.

After a few months more Mobasher looked upon Khaled and Said almost like sons. He could never feel the way he'd felt about Nouredine, that emotion had been extinguished from his life, but maybe they could help to fill it in part, until he was blessed with grandsons. After a year of sailing with them he even began to think they could become part of his family. His eldest daughter was too old for them, she was unattractive and not likely to attract many suitors, unless he could afford a dowry. But his two younger daughters were beautiful, like their mother, and Mobasher was beginning to think these boys might be suitors. He didn't think their families had gold, silver or land but he could see that both Khaled and Said were hard-working, and more importantly they seemed to have good hearts. The thought of his beloved daughters marrying men who turned out to be cruel caused Mobasher to lay awake at night.

Mobasher could not speak to them about this plan, even after a year of getting to know them and beginning to like them more. Little could he know that they were even beginning to think along the same lines. At the end of each fishing trip, Mobasher would be met in the harbour by his wife and daughters. They were there to help with sorting the catch and placing it in baskets that could be loaded onto a cart they would take to the fish traders in the Kasbah. The girls would never look at Khaled and Said directly, preferring to look down at the ground to show their modesty. But as sixteen and eighteen year-old boys they were now very aware of the beauty of women. In fact, seeing Mobasher's daughters at the end of sailing and fishing became the best part of their day.

As they walked home they could share their thoughts.

"They are truly beautiful, do you think we could marry and lay with wives like that, Khaled?"

Even the normally tough Khaled occasionally showed a softer, warmer side.

"Aisha is so beautiful, I would worship her all my days. Please Allah, let her be my wife."

For the moment they had to keep their desires between themselves, agreeing to say nothing to anyone, certainly not Mobasher, until they had made something of themselves and were worthy to be husbands for the two daughters of their master.

Khaled and Said became inseparable, brothers who would go jointly to sea with Mobasher every day if they could. Their primary aim was to learn how to sail but they also became proficient fishermen, which pleased their families, as they were paid a small amount of money from the proceeds of the day's catch, as well as a share of each catch, enough to feed them and their families.

At the end of a hot day in 1616 the two boys had finished working for Mobasher and the catch was so big it took longer than normal to unload and get to the market, where it would be sold the next day. They felt good as they made their way from the harbour through the narrow streets of Algiers to their homes, knowing their mothers would be delighted to see them each carrying a thin stick, from which six fish hung. They also had some small coins they could contribute towards the costs of their homes, thereby pleasing their fathers.

Both of them had been warned to be careful of the narrow streets as it got dark, the time when street gangs would appear and it wasn't considered safe. Aware of this but not afraid they made their way at a brisk walk and as they climbed the little streets between the houses it got darker. The atmosphere became tense and they could feel each other's nervousness, even if neither was willing to mention it. Then two young men stepped out from a doorway to stand directly in front of them, each holding a large stick threateningly.

"Good evening boys. Ah, it's the Morisco and his Berber brother."

Neither Said nor Khaled recognised them, not helped by the failing light. They stopped five steps short of the two young men and turned to retreat back the way they came, confident they could out run them. Unfortunately, behind them two more older boys stepped out of another doorway, one holding a knife, the other a club. Trapped in the narrow street they could call for help but by the time anyone came they could be laying in a pool of blood.

"We will take your catch, as well as any coins in your pockets."

"Our mothers need this to feed our families," Said pleaded with their leader.

One of the young men walked from behind and tried to take the stick from Said, but at sixteen he was not willing to lose the prize of a day's work and grappled with the bigger, older boy. In the struggle the sharp end of the stick pierced the arm of Said's attacker, causing him to let out a cry of pain. At that the other one who was behind Said came and dealt him a heavy blow to his back, causing Said to fall to the ground but still clutching his stick and attached fish.

"No, you can't."

Said began to appeal but was interrupted by the first one who had spoken and who appeared to be the leader.

"Here let me help you."

However, instead of assisting Said he meant to help him let go of the stick. The leader walked up and kicked Said with as much force as he could in the young boy's stomach, causing him a searing pain and loss of breath. Said doubled up and was choking for breath but it was about to get worse as all four closed in on him, including the one with the knife.

To this point Khaled had been an observer and the four attackers seemed to forget about him for a moment as they all focused on Said. Then as they were moving in to finish Said, the one with the knife fell to his knees with only a groan, Khaled struck with all his might using a large piece of wood that had been leaning against the wall. The one with the knife had been at the back of the pack of wolves closing in on Said, so they didn't see Khaled's attack but turned as they heard the groan and it was the leader who was next as Khaled brought the improvised club across his face with such force that the older boy's face was opened with the sound of his nose splitting. Blood poured as he fell holding his head, that felt and looked like it was exploding, dropping his weapon.

"Here, you can have this."

Khaled swung the boy's own club and brought it crashing against the side of the leader's head and he fell face first to the street without a sound. The other two had been frozen where they stood at the sight of the speed and ferocity of Khaled's attack. They both stepped backwards not looking, which resulted in one of them stumbling, and seemingly before he'd reached the ground Khaled was upon him delivering another massive blow to the head. The fourth attacker had managed to disappear into a darkened doorway, looking on in horror at the brutality of the attack. Khaled looked up and could sense where the fourth one hid.

"Stay there and watch. See what happens if you attack us, street rat."

With that Khaled calmly turned and walked over to the third and last attacker who had fallen. The young man was in a state of semi-consciousness and was trying to get to his feet, wiping blood from his eyes. He didn't see Khaled's weapon as it smashed into his face a second time and after the fourth time he was unconscious. It wasn't clear which blow killed him but Khaled had rained down on him an assault of eight to ten blows, leaving his face unrecognisable.

Khaled looked up and moved over to the other two attackers who lay on the ground and delivered three more blows to each of them. Three members of a street gang, who a short while before thought they would make light work of two boys, lay dead. All the time the fourth member of the gang had stood frozen in silence, shivering with fear, and finally Khaled, covered in the blood of the other three, turned to him.

"Go on, you can go now."

As the fourth failed assailant turned and ran away down the narrow street towards the harbour, Khaled turned to see Said, who had recovered from the kick to his stomach and watched the slaughter from street-level leaning on one elbow. He was speechless, it was the first time he had seen his friend and brother fight so viciously, and he wasn't to know then that it wouldn't be the last.

Khaled threw his weapon to the ground, picked up the sticks with the fish still attached with one hand, and helped his friend to his feet with the other.

"Come little brother, let's get away from here."

They made their way up through the streets, finding a horse trough to clean off as much blood as possible. Their mothers were relieved to see them and pleased to see the fish.

"Said, where have you been? It's getting dark and is dangerous at this time of the evening."

"Yes mother, I'm sorry."

In bed that night Said thought about what had happened, how Khaled had saved his life. His stomach still ached from the kick he had received and he could still see the face of the young man he had wrestled with, trying to keep hold of the fish. But it was the Khaled's face as he finished off the three attackers that appeared clearest in his mind. His brave friend, who had saved him, had shown no fear and proved he could kill a man. What struck Said most was Khaled had a look on his face which suggested that he had enjoyed his work in the Algiers backstreet that evening.

Mobasher

The rest of that year passed peacefully for Said and Khaled. They became more and more important to Mobasher and his family, as the old man was getting weary of going out on his boat every day. He came to trust in the two young men, even being happy to have them return to him each day after selling the catch at the market and handing over the profit. In return he paid them more, why not, they were doing all the work, and Said and Khaled found they were able to support their families, even saving some gold and silver, which they kept with a Jewish merchant called Isaac, in the Algiers' Old Town. This had been Said's idea but Khaled was not totally confident about this arrangement.

"What if he runs off with our gold and silver, Said?"

"Don't worry Khaled. Why should he do that and where would he go? He makes his money lending money and charging interest, and he is very successful and secure here in Algiers. He cannot go to Spain or Portugal, from where his people were expelled. In the rest of Europe Jews are treated like dogs, except in England and that's because they were expelled from there over 300 years ago. They allow no Jews. Here Isaac is protected by the Grand Pasha and throughout the Ottoman Empire Jews are protected by the Sultan. Isaac and his people are safe providing they pay their taxes."

Khaled found himself nodding in agreement with his younger, wiser friend.

"How do you know all this Said?"

"Because I listen to people who are wiser than me Khaled, I try to learn from them."

Khaled recognised this as a quality that his younger friend had that he himself did not possess.

The pair were also becoming important to Mobasher's family through their relationship with his younger daughters, Aisha and Alya. With Mobasher doing less and less in the family business, he was happy for the two girls to go and help with the unloading of the fish and their sale to a merchant at the market. This was a way of keeping an eye on the two boys, the size of the catch and the income from its sale. Mobasher was happy to let the girls go alone, knowing Said and Khaled would escort them home. He trusted the boys and hoped they would become fond of his daughters, eventually becoming part of his family.

This development in relations was of mutual benefit and enjoyed by the four young people. At sea with no-one around the day would pass with Khaled and Said talking about Aisha and Alya. Their intentions were honourable and Khaled's language, his words and the tone of his voice, were different from the way he spoke about the slave girls they saw in the market. Said was pleased with this change in Khaled's attitude towards women. Now they were like brothers and if they married Mobasher's daughters, they would become family, with their children being cousins and growing up together.

Fifteen months later, Khaled and Said were twenty and eighteen years old, young but experienced fishermen and increasingly wealthy. They even considered buying their own boat, which made commercial sense, as they would keep all of the profit, instead of giving it to Mobasher. This was discussed many times at sea, where they could both think and speak freely, examining every aspect of what they might do. Because of their feelings for his daughters this option was carefully considered but always, by mutual agreement, decided against.

"Once we marry them the boat will be effectively ours and he's been good to us. I do not want to see him suffer in any way."

Said was pleased to hear these words from his friend, given that he had a street reputation for cold brutality, ever since that night two years ago. But when it came to Mobasher's family his intentions were completely honourable.

"I agree Khaled. We can continue to help Mobasher and with the gold and silver we save, we can buy another boat."

"Who would sail it Said?"

"We can take charge of a boat each and hire young seamen, just as Mobasher hired us."

Again, Khaled nodded and listened as Said laid-out their commercial future.

"If we help young men, like Mobasher helped us, why should we not have three, four, or more fishing boats. Eventually, we could send them out in the morning and be there when they return, take the fish to market, sell it and prosper. We should pay our men well so they are not tempted to steal or cheat. You and I would be there when they return and there's no-one in Algiers who doesn't know of your reputation, Khaled."

Khaled's eyes widened and a big smile appeared across his face.

"Said, you have a great mind, I think you should have been a rich merchant."

"Ha, ha, perhaps I will be one day Khaled. I will need you with me though."

Said gave Khaled a friendly shove that almost saw him topple over the side of the boat, but Said grabbed his hand, pulling him to the middle. The two young men laughed together, as they had done for more than eight years and sailed back to Algiers, full of optimism for the future.

They entered the harbour and moored the small fishing boat in the usual place. There to help them were Aisha and Alya, their heads covered but not their faces as was the custom in some countries. Said and Khaled had heard of such customs in some Muslim countries far to the east, beyond Istanbul, but were pleased that it wasn't the case in Algiers. Although Mobasher's daughters knew the two young men well they always kept their distance, showing modesty and respect. However, occasionally the two girls could be caught glancing at them as they worked, causing them such embarrassment that they quickly looked away.

To see the two maidens smile was the greatest pleasure Said and Khaled experienced at this time. The thought of looking into the eyes of one of them as their wife, in the privacy of their own bedroom, was a thought that made them think of paradise. Khaled was more passionate about this happening than his young friend and he thought about it more each day. His love for Aisha had grown more intense as the months passed.

The duties of unloading the catch and getting the fish to the market was done with goodwill and humour that evening, followed by Khaled and Said escorting Aisha and Alya back to their father's house. They always let the girls lead the way, respectfully following three paces behind. Occasionally there might be a pause and Khaled was quick to ask if there was a problem.

"Are you well Aisha, do you need some water?"

Aisha glanced at Alya amused. Then turning her head replied with the same beautiful smile, before carrying on with the walk.

"Thank you Khaled, I will be fine. I'm not a little girl you know."

Khaled knew that he was not being admonished, and glanced sideways to see Said trying to suppress laughter. Khaled didn't care, there was nowhere else he'd rather be. There was no-one else he'd rather be with, than these three people he loved.

That evening Khaled and Said walked home happy with life, without speaking they shared the same thoughts. They would keep helping and working for Mobasher, they would soon have Aisha and Alya as their wives. Together they would prosper, brothers providing for their families.

It wasn't clear what time it happened but it was certainly after nightfall. Screaming and shouting woke everyone in their houses but it was uncertain what the alarm was for. Said got up and dressed, making his way out of his house to find-out what was wrong. He could see others emerging from their homes and turned to see the cause of the alarm. Fire lit up the sky and he immediately realised it was close to the home of Mobasher. Without waiting he ran down the street in the direction of the flames rising into the sky.

He arrived at a scene of chaos and carnage, people running in all directions, many of them not going anywhere but simply screaming and crying. Some were crying from the pain of burnt flesh, others from desperation and grief. There he found Mobasher, his skin blackened from smoke, his face blank.

"Mobasher, where are they? Where are Alya and Aisha?"

Mobasher looked at Said but didn't seem to recognise him, his face a picture of shock.

"They're gone, my babies, they're all gone." With that the old man sank to his knees and held his head in his hands. Moments later Khaled arrived.

"Where's Aisha? Tell me she's alive."

Said couldn't speak as he stared at the inferno, which was so hot no-one could get within twenty steps. He then turned to Khaled and shook his head. Khaled's look was of total disbelief and he tried to approach the burning house screaming.

"Aisha, Aisha!"

He had to turn back short of the flames that scorched his face and hair. His reaction was different to Said's and his emotions took over.

"No, no. Aisha, please Allah, let her not be in there."

With that he let out a scream from deep inside his body and like Mobasher before him he sank to his knees. Said walked over, leaned down enveloping his friend in his arms and tears fell from his eyes.

"We've lost them Khaled, they're gone."

There was no way of extinguishing the blaze and the three men could do no more than sit and watch it burn itself out. A line of five homes had been destroyed. By the time the sun had risen the fire had burned for four or five hours and all that was left of the houses were stones, bricks and charred wood. Neighbours had tried to comfort Mobasher but there was nothing they could say to alleviate his grief. Eventually the remains of the girls, their older sister and mother were found. They were unrecognisable but they were four women and they were buried together later that day. Their burial was sombre, no women attended so there was no loud wailing, just the three men. Mobasher was silent, still in a state of shock, he had to be supported by Said and Khaled, as he threw dirt onto their covered corpses. Said and Khaled then used spades to shovel the dry red soil onto the four women. For the first and only time, Said saw tears flow from Khaled's eyes.

Trying to establish what caused the fire was futile but it was believed to be cooking oil overheating and igniting close to fabrics that were hanging to dry in one of the houses. Mobasher had been out speaking to an Iman about what needed to be done if his daughters were to marry Said and Khaled. He got home as the flames took hold of the line of houses but couldn't get in, all four women were probably overcome by smoke long before their bodies were destroyed by the flames, or so their father hoped.

In the days after the fire Said and Khaled were at a loss for what to do. There was nothing to say, both of the young men dealt with their loss in their own way. Said was thoughtful and tried to make sense of what had happened, how it had happened, considering whether it was anyone's fault. He concluded no-one was to blame, it was simply a tragedy, Allah had chosen to take the girls from this world. However, Khaled was different, his overwhelming emotion was anger, how could his beautiful Aisha be taken from him. He alternated between tears and fury that became a rage that left him wanting to make someone or something pay. It was exhausting and eventually he was left feeling empty, devoid of emotion. Any love he was capable of showing a woman was ripped from his heart that night. He vowed he would never again be vulnerable to affection.

For Mobasher it was worse, he was an old man who had lost everything. The house was destroyed but that could be replaced, unlike his beloved family. He wandered the streets for several days, without appetite for food or drink. When he eventually had to rest he found himself down at the harbour and climbed into his boat, lay down and slept for two days. He would've chosen to never wake up but was found by Said who, after a couple of days of grieving, thought of the old man and realised he might need some help.

"Mobasher, here I've brought you some water and food. You must eat and drink."

The old man looked up, his face drawn and etched with pain. He looked ten years older than he had five days earlier.

"Thank you Said, but I don't want to eat or drink. My life is over."

Said stayed with Mobasher for the rest of the morning. They talked about the girls and how much joy they brought to them both. Mobasher seemed to improve his state of mind and even ate and drank some water. They sat in the fishing boat together in their grief and eventually Said felt he could leave the old man for a while.

"Where will you live Mobasher?"

"I will sleep here in my boat. It's all I have left."

"Come to my house, we can make space and take care of you."

Said knew he and Khaled could pay for somewhere for Mobasher from the gold and silver they had saved with Isaac.

"Said, you and Khaled have been like sons to me. Thank you, but I will stay here."

Said agreed, thinking with blankets and a canvas the boat would be enough for now. Besides, he couldn't force the old man. He would return later in the early evening with more food, water and blankets to make the boat more comfortable for sleeping. In his mind he was thinking this might work, everyone down at the harbour knew Mobasher and could keep an eye on him. Khaled and he could get back to fishing and look after him.

"I will be back later Mobasher, stay here."

It was late morning and Said went back into town to find Khaled, let him know about the situation of Mobasher, get food, water and other provisions to take back to the old man. After some searching he found his friend, who he hadn't seen for several days as they'd left each other to grieve. Khaled wasn't interested in anything at first, but eventually he overcame his own self-pity to think about Mobasher and his loss. The two friends worked together again to try and help the old man. By the late afternoon they had a cartload of provisions and made their way down to the harbour, but neither Mobasher or the boat were there.

Mobasher had sat in the boat for an hour or so after Said left. It was good of the boy who he had hoped would one day be his son, to care and try to look after him. But despite the kindness of Said, his mind was set. For the last time Mobasher sailed out of Algiers harbour into the great bay. Feeling the sea wind on his face, he was able to forget his sorrow for a short while and remembered how it use to be, fishing and returning to his beautiful family. But now there was no family to return to, there was nothing to live for. Out in the Bay of Algiers he looked around at the sea and back at the great city one last time and thought about his girls. Without hesitation he tied a heavy weight to his waist, then holding it with both arms he stepped over the side of his boat.

The fishing boat was returned to Algiers by other fishermen who knew Mobasher. Without any firm evidence no-one could be certain of what happened but he had been seen sailing it out to sea and the boat was found empty and drifting. Said and Khaled came to the same conclusion as everyone else and they were correct. Mobasher was grief-stricken and had nothing to live for. They were saddened at the loss of the old man, who they were fond of, but couldn't blame him for taking his own life.

For some days both Said and Khaled were at a loss for what to do, heart-broken at the deaths of Alya and Aisha, as well as losing any appetite for work. The gold and silver they had saved meant they didn't need to work every day and the purpose of their labour no longer existed. They met each day and talked about the girls and what they should do next. After a week of mourning and lethargy they decided it was time to get on with life and agreed a plan together.

"We can keep fishing Said. Mobasher would want us to keep his boat and no-one else has laid claim to it. We can work well together and we will keep all of the profits."

"Yes, we should do that Khaled, but what about the future. Do you want to be a fisherman for the rest of your life?"

It was a prospect they both accepted when they were thinking of married life but it was never their personal preference.

Khaled knew what Said was referring to, their ambitions to be Corsairs.

"We can go back to fishing for a while, maybe a year, then see if an opportunity arises to join a Corsair captain. We will have more gold and silver that we can save with Isaac. Khaled, I think we could learn the art of being Corsairs and eventually have our own galley. Then we could become rich."

As Said spoke Khaled stared out to sea. He knew he had to move on from the grief of losing Aisha and was always impressed by the big thoughts and ambitions of his younger friend. They talked late into the night and agreed to be partners, first as fishermen and eventually as Corsairs.

Abdul

For the next year the two friends worked tirelessly, fishing nearly every day, selling it at the market and saving as much as they could with Isaac. At the same time, they kept a close eye on the comings and goings of the galleys sailing out of Algiers, returning with captives and following closely when time permitted their sale at the market. They were particularly interested in the different captains, how they treated their crew and how they treated their captives. Each captain had his own style and after some months they came to identify two or three they would like to sail for.

It was about thirteen months after the death of the girls and Mobasher that they decided to approach one captain called Abdul the Turk, a large man well-known around Algiers for being firm but generous and fair. Men who worked under him knew of his skill as a sailor and a soldier, having no time for insubordination and laziness. But they knew that if they were disciplined and followed orders, Abdul was loyal and more generous when sharing the spoils of raids. The celebrations he would pay for, after a successful raid, were well-known throughout Algiers. Abdul was resting after returning from a successful raid that saw the capture of two small merchant ships and fifteen men taken straight to market for sale.

"Thank you for your request to join my crew. I have seen and heard about both of you. You look like fine young men but unfortunately, I do not need any new Corsairs at the moment. If I do I will find you."

With that Abdul turned and walked into town. Said looked at Khaled and shrugged his shoulders.

"So, we can wait a while longer."

Four weeks later as they were unloading the catch for the day, the shadow of a large man appeared across the nets in the boat and Khaled, feeling a threat, turned drawing his dagger. A large man stepped back.

"Calm down Khaled, it's me, Abdul."

Realising who it was, Khaled was a little embarrassed and lowered his hand and dagger.

"I'm sorry Abdul, I didn't see you, but only felt your presence."

Khaled knew if Abdul had intended to hurt him, he would be dead by now, as the big Turk's reputation as a Corsair was known throughout the Ottoman Empire.

"That's good Khaled, I like your instincts and reactions. They could be useful."

Said had stood silent observing until this point.

"Hello Abdul, it is an honour to be visited by so famous a captain. May we ask why you've come to the fishing harbour?"

Said thought it could be for only one reason but didn't want to make any assumptions.

"I returned from a week at sea two days ago, during which we seized three ships but unfortunately one of them had soldiers who put up a fight. All seven of them were killed but we lost three men. After thinking about whether to replace them, I could manage with the remaining eleven Corsairs in my crew, I then remembered two strong, eager, young men offering their services only recently."

Smiles appeared on the faces of Said and Khaled, to which Abdul responded with a loud laugh.

"So do you think you could be Corsairs?"

It was an unnecessary question, as Abdul could see from the joy on their faces what the answer would be. A conversation followed about sailing, weapons, fighting and payments, after which Abdul told them to meet him at his galley in ten days. He liked to relax after a week at sea, particularly if it had been fruitful. This meant he would eat well, drink wine and enjoy his favourite women at a brothel owned by a friend in the Old Town.

No longer boys sailing a fishing boat with Mobasher, Khaled and Said set sail as young men and part of the Corsair crew captained by Abdul the Turk. They were immediately valued as excellent sailors and were told to stay at Abdul's side as his personal guards. There they could watch the experienced men board the first ship seized and how captives were taken.

"I don't want men who are overcome with blood-lust and start slaying everyone on the ship. The captives are useless, or should I say worthless, to us if they are killed. If men fight back, we kill a few, putting fear into the hearts of the rest. This should be enough, seamen and passengers on ships are not normally warriors."

Said listened carefully to everything Abdul said. He was impressed by Abdul's calm approach, who sounded more like a man running a business than a pirate. His admiration increased even more when he saw the first ship taken and captives seized, as it went exactly as Abdul predicted, with an initial resistance by the crew halted by the killing of two of them who had grabbed their swords. The eight remaining crew fell into line and were quickly put in chains. Said looked at Khaled and nodded his admiration. Khaled smiled and they shared the same thought. This is exactly what they wanted to do.

On the same voyage another ship was seized and five more captives taken, without any bloodshed, making it a successful ten days at sea. Some goods of value were also taken and the small cargo ship was sunk without trace. They returned to Algiers and saw the thirteen captives taken straight to the slave market. Abdul couldn't have been happier with the outcome and was able to pay his Corsairs handsomely, including Khaled and Said. The two friends rested for a couple of days, as ten days at sea was always tiring due to unsettled sleep, then returned to fishing until they heard again from Abdul. However, immediately after that first voyage with Abdul, they both knew fishing was not going to be their work for much longer. It was more regular and less tiring but it had none of the thrill and excitement of chasing and capturing a Christian ship.

After a few weeks passed they were called to join Abdul again, then repeatedly as trusted crewmen. Within a year Khaled and Said had become experienced Corsairs, sailing with Abdul ten to twelve times. The Turkish captain came to like and value the two young men. Khaled was a fierce fighter and Said was intelligent and trustworthy. Abdul eventually had confidence in Said to deal with the slave merchants in the market, which usually resulted in the young Morisco returning with more gold and silver than he had expected, or thought he would've secured if he'd gone himself.

"Ah Said, how have we got on, how much did we make?"

Abdul's question was usually the same and was met by Said and Khaled placing the gold and silver on the table, followed by celebrations enjoyed by all of the crew. These celebrations would usually involve enjoying the company of women from the whore houses in the Old Town, which Said tried but didn't particularly enjoy, in contrast to Khaled, who developed an appetite for women of all colours, taken from all corners of Africa and Europe. On such nights Said would leave Khaled to his pleasure, go home to sleep and find his friend a day or two later.

Khaled and Said worked like this for Abdul for five years, their days as fishermen ending within the first year, with them selling off their boat. They became his best and most trusted Corsairs, just as they had become trusted and relied on by Mobasher. This time there were no daughters of Abdul's who by marrying they could become family. However, Abdul was becoming tired of the life of chasing Christian ships and taking captives. An astute businessman he knew the life of a Corsair was not always long, as Christian warships, particularly from Spain, were always hunting the likes of him. Christian religious orders like the Trinitarians knew of him and his head carried a reward. In the last of these five years he became more nervous and began to think of a way out of his life as a Corsair. He could stay in Algiers and enjoy life but there was always the danger of someone wanting the reward on his head. If he stopped going to sea he would no longer have the income to employ Corsairs who served as his guards.

Abdul liked both Khaled and Said but it was the latter that he respected for his intelligence, which led him to talk to Said about this predicament.

"So you see Said, I do not want to continue for much longer. It is a great life for a man in his prime but not for a man who is getting old."

"What and where would you like to go Abdul?"

"I think I would like to return to Istanbul Said. It is a wonderful city of hundreds of thousands, where I have family, and a man with wealth can live anonymously and certainly secure from any Christians seeking his head for reward."

Said nodded and understood. Algiers was safe from the Spanish at the moment but perhaps it would not always be. Then there were the Italians, French, Portuguese and even the English. All of these countries and states had good reason to attack Corsairs. Whereas Istanbul would always be safe and Abdul explained that provided he paid taxes the great Sultan would offer protection no-one dared breach.

Abdul and Said returned to the conversation several times and began to develop a plan that would provide Abdul with a way out and would be of mutual benefit to Khaled and Said.

"Abdul, let us buy your main galley and your bagno. We have saved gold and silver, which we have kept safe with the money-lender Isaac. If it is not enough, you have my word we will save more and get it to you in Istanbul over the next year or two."

Said knew they had more than enough for the big galley, on which they'd served for nearly five years. He loved the ship and knew it inside out. Captaining it would be straightforward with a good crew, he'd watched Abdul do it for over four years. The bagno was another matter. This large building, in which captives were kept in Algiers, was something he hadn't thought about before but it seemed a great opportunity. They wouldn't be just Corsairs taking captives straight to market, they could take them to their bagno and choose the time to sell that suited them. Some captives could be kept for use as oarsmen on their galley, some taken to market, some women sold immediately, the most beautiful kept until wealthy harem owners visited the Algiers slave market.

To the delight of Khaled and Said, Abdul liked the idea. He and Said agreed a fair price for both sides and additionally a way of getting Abdul to Istanbul safely. A small, fast galley manned by Corsairs and slaves would take him there and the Corsairs would be paid handsomely on their return with proof of Abdul's safe passage. Even Abdul's gold and silver would be safe, in fact it wouldn't leave Algiers but be swapped for the same amount through Isaac's family in Istanbul. The wealthy Jew was part of a family that provided finance and helped countries trade in every corner of the Mediterranean, whether they be Christian or Muslim.

By the end of 1625 Khaled and Said were the owners of a large galley, two smaller ones and importantly a bagno in Algiers. Their bagno was one of the smaller ones and could house fifteen to twenty Corsairs, as well as up to 100 slaves. There were much larger ones belonging to men like the Pasha that could hold up to a thousand slaves, but that didn't bother Khaled and Said. They were fully operational as Corsair slavers, just ten years after they had decided it was their ambition, when as boys they use to sit on the harbour wall watching galleys setting forth and returning laden with human cargoes.

Mevagissey

The fishing village of Mevagissey in Cornwall, sat in a small bay and was protected by a sea-wall, built and rebuilt by its residents over the centuries. It was nothing like the great sea walls of larger towns but offered enough protection to the small number of boats owned by the fishing families of the village from storms and their furious waves. Every family in the village had contributed in some way over the years to building and maintaining the wall, it had become a proud symbol of the village in which they felt safe.

With the sea and surrounding fertile land every family was able to support itself, if they were well enough to work. The wealth they created supported local tradesman and a tavern. At the centre of the village was the small Norman church, which was important to the whole community. The minister and his churchwarden were responsible for delivering poor relief to any families and individuals who found themselves in extreme poverty and unable to support themselves. This role of the parish was the same in Mevagissey as everywhere else in England, as the old Queen had passed laws that made it the responsibility of the parish to raise money through rates charged to those who could afford to pay, which was to be used to provide poor relief to the 'deserving poor' who needed it. Elizabeth's Poor Law even required each parish to provide a 'place of habitation' for those with no home, so every parish had its own poor house or workhouse. It was preferred if possible for the poor to stay in their own homes and receive poor relief but sometimes a roof over their heads was required.

Mevagissey had a small cottage where paupers could be housed if required. However in 1631 the villagers were proud of the little cottage being empty for the last year or two. Seventeen years before Laura Baddow had been born in that cottage and it was her home for almost the first year of her life. Laura's mother, Mary, had come to the village on foot, carrying a small bag and the heavy emotional load of a child in her womb. Barely eighteen years of age Mary had been made pregnant by an older man in the town of Falmouth, where she had lived with her family. Charmed and then seduced by the older man, her honesty prevented her from saying it was rape. This was possibly a mistake on Mary's part, as the shame of an unmarried pregnant daughter might have been accepted by her father if the child was conceived against her will. Unfortunately, Mary's innocence in these matters meant she faced the full shame and anger of her father. She was cast out of the family home and told to leave the town. They didn't want to see her and her bastard on the streets of Falmouth.

After walking for three days Mary came across Mevagissey in the spring of 1613. With a gale coming in off the sea, she was soaking wet from driving rain. The young girl couldn't continue, needed shelter and found an alcove in the outside wall of the village church, just as the sun disappeared and the village fell into darkness. She was found the next morning by the minister huddled into an alcove which 100 years earlier, before the Reformation, had housed a statue of the Virgin Mary. The irony of this wasn't lost on the vicar and may have saved her.

The church vestry faced a dilemma over what to do about the girl. It was normal practise and required by law to return vagabonds to their parish of origin. She was Falmouth's responsibility and Megavissey rate payers, like those in every parish, did not warm to paying rates to support the poor of the next parish, never mind a town many miles away, or even worse, immigrants from Ireland.

Mary was in a desperate state and couldn't be driven out of the village, as both she and the unborn child would perish. She was placed in the village poor house, with blankets, some food and a lit fire. It remained to be seen if she would survive her ordeal. At the resulting vestry meeting the vicar, churchwarden and five family heads representative of the parish discussed what to do with the girl. They were all aware of the law but knew her future would be bleak if she was returned to Falmouth. The women who tended to her, getting her out of the sodden clothes she wore and dressing her in replacement items of their own, were able to report to the men in the vestry that there was no known father and she had been disowned by her family. If she was lucky she would end up in the larger Falmouth poor house but she might go astray and end up a street whore in the port, where she would sell her body to support her child.

Fortunately for Mary, the isolation of the village away from interfering politicians and the kindness of the villagers, resulted in her being allowed to stay. A few of the rate payers might have resented paying for the pregnant girl, but the overwhelming majority were happy to help and any dissenters were shamed into silence by appeals to the parish members' Christian conscience.

Four months later Laura was born on a sunny day in July and baptised two days later in the church, where Mary had sought shelter on her first night in Mevagissey. To protect them both from the past Mary had agreed with the minister to register the child simply with the name "Laura", her mother "Mary, a pauper," father "Unknown."

Mary recovered from the birth, Laura thrived and they were simply known as the girl Mary and her child. Initially she wouldn't leave the small cottage, the shame of being an unmarried mother confining her indoors, but eventually the women who visited persuaded her she must go out for the health of the child. Mary knew this was true, eventually venturing down to the harbour and nearby beach, all the time conscious of staring eyes and unable to look anyone in the face. The kind greetings of the villagers were met with "Thank you Sir", or "Thank you Ma'am", always looking to the ground as she held Laura close. It wasn't ideal but Mary knew the parish vestry had saved her and Laura.

Like paupers in poor houses across England, Mary was given work to do and she proved to be a skilled seamstress, making simple but strong, dependable clothes. Working through the autumn and winter Mary showed she could be an asset to the village with the skills she'd learnt from her grandmother put to good use. In the spring of 1614, one year after arriving in Mevagissey, Mary and Laura moved out of the parish poor house into a small cottage of their own, rented from one of the local wealthy families.

With an income from work and independence from parish poor relief, Mary felt happy and came to love this village that had taken her in. She saw her future there in Mevagissey with security for her and Laura. In that summer of 1614 she could reflect on what had happened over the previous two years and life for her and Laura began to look hopeful. 'Maybe one day I might become a ratepayer, contributing to the poor relief of others, as these people have done for me,' she thought. This was certainly becoming a possibility, as despite being an outsider Mary began to feel accepted, her clothes becoming popular with many families in the village and surrounding farms. Women would recommend her to neighbours.

"The girl Mary could make that for you. She has a gift for making clothes."

Even wealthier families would turn to her, rather than go to a town.

"Just give her the cloth material and she will make a beautiful dress for your Sarah's wedding."

However, there was one problem stopping Mary being totally accepted by the other women, which meant she couldn't be trusted, particularly by those women who were not old. It was nothing to do with her character and the reason was plain to see. Mary was attractive, maybe not beautiful, but pleasing to the eye of any man. Barely nineteen years of age, she would always dress modestly, her head covered and wearing plain clothes but she would always turn the heads of men.

"Look at her, she should be married."

"I agree Sarah, and if she doesn't our men will always be admiring her."

It was true and in the tavern after drinking ale men would think what a few of them would say.

"My God, look at that girl, she is a beauty and should be keeping a man warm at night."

"Aye, wish it was me."

It was a common reply, usually said with humour drawing laughter, often a thinly veiled expression of secret desire.

Mary was aware of the predicament she was in and felt uncomfortable in the company of more than one or two people, never allowing herself to be anywhere alone with men. She didn't desire a husband, she was too busy working and caring for Laura. Alone at night she did sometimes wonder if she could she be loved by a man and not just desired. But her experience as a maid left her thinking she was not destined for happiness with a man.

To preserve what remained of her reputation Mary did everything she could to avoid the stares of men, never going out after dark and always locking her doors securely. A knock at the door after dark would be ignored, pretending to be asleep. Aware of the admiring glances, she knew it would always be an issue that prevented her from being a friend of the women. Life continued like this for three years and whilst Mary felt secure, the problem remained.

Everything changed in the spring of 1618. Having been to church that Sunday morning Mary was working on the vegetable garden at the back of her cottage. She didn't have to do this as she was making enough money from her work to pay rent and buy food she and Laura needed. However, Mary was aware that to not tend her garden and grow some vegetables would be seen as arrogant by other women in the village. Everyone grew as much as they could, even the wealthier families. Planting and tending to her small patch of land was something she had been intending to do for a while, at least the sun was shining and it was warm enough to allow Laura to run around and play. So, Mary set about the shared ritual of planting and growing food, at least in that respect she could be like the other women.

"Good morning Miss Mary."

Mary had been leaning over digging a small furrow in the soil, into which she would place a line of seeds. Four words from a man's voice made her freeze and she stayed still, staring down at the soil, not knowing whether to look up.

"I'm sorry for disturbing you Miss Mary. Please tell me to leave if my presence is unacceptable or offends you."

Not wanting to be seen to be ill-mannered, Mary got to her feet, shielding her eyes from the sun with her hand. The man before her was someone she recognised from church but didn't know by name, making it likely he was from a nearby hamlet or farm.

"Good morning Sir, have I done something wrong?"

"No, no Miss Mary, please do not be alarmed. There is nothing wrong. I wanted to call and pay my respects to you. It is a beautiful day."

He appeared to be a polite gentleman, which made her a little less nervous, but she had known a 'so-called' gentleman four years ago, which led to her predicament.

"Yes Sir, it is a fine day."

Mary replied but could think of nothing else to say, so they stood and looked at each other in silence for what seemed an eternity.

"Thank you, Miss Mary. I hope you and your daughter enjoy the rest of this beautiful Sunday."

With that the man turned to leave but somehow Mary had the presence of mind to speak.

"Excuse me Sir, you know my name but I do not know yours."

The man blushed with embarrassment.

"I am so sorry Miss Mary, please forgive my lack of manners. I am John Baddow."

He nodded respectfully, turned and left. Mary stood and watched him walk away and wondered what was happening. When he was out of sight she returned to working the soil and thought about it.

John Baddow's visit had not gone unnoticed. A while later as Mary was tidying up after her labour, her neighbour Claire came over. A kind woman, Claire was old enough to be Mary's mother. She sympathised with the young unmarried mother and her husband John was even older, safe from temptation.

"Well Mary, a visit from a man like John Baddow is a welcome interruption to working the soil in your vegetable garden."

Claire had lived in Mevagissey all of her fifty-two years and knew everyone in the village, the surrounding hamlets and farms for ten miles. She, like most of the older women in the village knew all of the families in the area, who was married to who, who was whose cousin, who was engaged to who and who was in the family way. Even if Claire did not know everyone personally, she had a good idea of who they were and what they did, which was just the case with John Baddow. It was only Mary's modesty and her limited experience of the wider world that accounted for her not knowing of his circumstances.

John Baddow was a tall, strong, handsome man, a farmer thirty years of age, living just two miles outside of Mevagissey. Sadly those details were not those with which most people identified him him. He had two children aged eight and six, but he should've had three children and a wife. Two years earlier his dear wife Matilda died in childbirth, along with a daughter who was never baptised, buried without a name. The story of poor Matilda was known as it was such a shock to everyone. She was a well-proportioned woman, strong enough to hold a plough and had given birth to their son and daughter without problems.

"She'll give him six or eight children."

Women would say after the birth of their second.

"Aye, and then she'll be in the field the next day."

Unfortunately for them both the baby had not turned in her womb and despite all the efforts of a local woman skilled in midwifery, the unborn infant would not turn. No-one had expected any problems but the labour became an ordeal, sapping Matilda of all her strength. After her repeated attempts to move the baby, the labour got worse as Matilda started to bleed and there was no way to stop it. Matilda became ever weaker and the birth became critical, it had to happen or mother and child would be lost. Finally, the baby appeared but it was limp and wouldn't breathe; the struggle for life had proved too much for the little bundle that was already blue in colour. The umbilical cord was wrapped around its tiny neck.

"No wonder it didn't turn, it was already dead in her womb, poor thing."

Worse, the woman could see the condition of Matilda was deteriorating as she continued to bleed, despite best efforts to staunch the flow of blood. Less than one hour after the delivery of the baby, Matilda had lost so much blood she couldn't survive. The midwives brought John into the bedroom to see his beloved wife once more before she was gone. Her eyes were barely open and she couldn't say any more than one word.

"Sorry."

John held his wife's hand as tears fell down his cheeks, and he watched her breathe her last breath. After a while the midwives came in and asked him to leave so they could take care of Matilda. As he got up John could see the blood-soaked sheets that told him all he needed to know about why they both died. He broke down in tears at the thought of the pain Matilda must have suffered, it should've been him saying sorry.

Matilda was buried with her baby and John was faced with life without the woman he'd thought would always be there as a wife he adored, the mother to his six-year-old son and four-year-old daughter.

For the first year after Matilda's death John was busy with the farm and providing for his children. After about eighteen months he realised he missed Matilda but he also missed having a wife and companion. It was then that he thought about the possibility of finding a new wife and it was also the time that he began to see Mary and her daughter in church every Sunday morning. At first, he just noticed her as a mother without a husband but as the weeks passed by he couldn't help looking at her more and see that, despite dressing in the plainest clothes and always covering much of her face, she was an attractive woman.

After initially noticing how pleasing she was to his eye, John found himself thinking about Mary more and more, particularly at the end of the day when he was alone. The person he spoke to first was his mother and she knew of the young woman who had arrived in the village. An unmarried mother at the age of eighteen came with a damaged reputation but his mother had also heard how the girl had managed to stand on her on two feet after spending a year in the parish poor house, earning the respect of many of the older women. Indeed, she had been impressed with the young woman's manners when she employed her services to make a dress. Mary was now twenty-two years-old, the perfect age for marriage and could give John more children.

Anne Baddow thought about the matter and had no hesitation in giving him her support. She knew her son needed and deserved a wife, to help him with the farm and the children, but also as a companion who could keep him warm at night. So, it was after a few more months of thinking about it and eventually plucking up enough courage that John approached Mary as she tended her vegetable garden. Anne was beginning to lose patience.

"Have you paid your respects to the girl Mary yet?"

Anne would ask him each Sunday evening. It was with great relief that he finally replied on that Sunday in March 1618.

"Yes mother, I have."

"Well, what did she say?"

They were a good match, Mary was twenty-two, John was thirty, both healthy and able to have more children if they wanted. Their marriage was in October that same year and Mary's only stipulation was that John would take Laura as his own daughter. She didn't need to worry, John had assumed that would be natural and a duty he must perform as a husband and a father. They had a courtship which was warm but also business-like. Both found the other attractive and, in their thoughts, wondered what it would be like to be intimate, but if that didn't prove to be successful it wasn't as important as them having a good marriage, supporting each other and raising their children in a secure home.

For the first time since discovering she was pregnant five years previously, Mary could feel truly happy and secure. Life in the rented cottage for her and Laura was good and the village and its people were kind to them. But there was always something missing and now John Baddow filled that space.

Moving two miles to a bigger house, with land and animals was not difficult, even if for Mary there was a little apprehension and uncertainty. At the age of four there were no reservations for Laura, as she soon realised that the man she would come to know as father was kind and treated her as his own. Furthermore, life for Laura immediately became more interesting with her acquiring an older brother and sister. James and Susan Baddow had been heartbroken at the loss of their mother two years earlier, but after time to grieve they were happy to find they would be getting a new mother when their father explained. They liked little Laura and the marriage of John and Mary gave them a mother who was hard-working and more importantly, kind to them. Just as John treated Laura as his own daughter, Mary treated James and Susan as her own.

Mary reflected on her life as she looked out across the farm. It seemed just months ago, not four years, since she'd wandered into Mevagissey, heavily pregnant with Laura. She thought about her own parents who had thrown her out of the family home, a young girl who'd made a simple but devastating mistake. As she did, she swore to herself she would never expel her own daughter, James or Susan. With John they were her family, more precious than anything and they were her reason for living. Mary was thankful and set about preparing dinner for her family.

Callum

Callum Longbow and Jack Cardet are at sea with five other men. The pair are the youngest but not the weakest of the crew, both fully grown, almost in their prime. Both tall but Jack is slim and well-defined in body shape. A handsome boy, he's popular with all of the young maids, who might be thinking who to dance with in the Maytime summer celebrations. Callum is as tall as Jack but has the body of a man twice his age, thick strong arms and legs, a chest like a bull. Perhaps he isn't as admired by as many of the maidens looking for a summer sweetheart, but his quiet, serious resolve appeals more to the girls who might be looking for a husband; a strong young man who would support and protect his family, and work hard without flagging.

The other men are older and in varying degrees of sea-weariness, which comes with experience and tired bodies. Two of them are possibly ten years older than Callum and Jack, both married with children. They go to sea now with less sense of adventure, unlike their two youngest sea-mates. With marriage and fatherhood comes responsibility and they need to make money. Then there are three older men, two are old seadogs who know no other life; on land they spend their time and money in taverns, their wives dead or gone, tired of their drunken husbands. The last member of the crew and oldest is the captain, James Weston, an experienced and fair man who local seamen were happy to sail with.

Captain Weston had known Jack's father for many years; they sailed together as boys under the command of Drake, when he led Elizabeth's fleet that routed the Spanish Armada. That was forty-three years ago and they had sailed together to many exotic places, even the Americas. Now James Weston was fifty-seven and he was looking for just one or two more big voyages to secure his retirement, during which he would watch his grandchildren grow, visit the tavern to enjoy good cider and the company of old friends. Sadly, that company could not include Jack's father, who was taken ill last Autumn, and confined to his bed he never left his house to gaze out to sea again. On visiting his old shipmate James Weston agreed to look out for Jack, as it was clear by then that the boy would follow in his father's footsteps and go to sea. Why not, it had served them well in seeing the world and allowed them to make sufficient to support a family.

Callum was Jack's close friend and he was part of the package that Captain Weston agreed to apprentice. Callum was a boy of modest family wealth, raised by his mother and grandmother as his father had died when he was young. Perhaps being fatherless endeared the two boys to Weston, who was not a sentimental fool but he had come to like them. He wouldn't let them, and certainly not the rest of the crew, see any fondness but he couldn't help but like them for their youthful enthusiasm, their strength, energy, and even their beauty. Sailing a ship a captain can spend a lot of time in quiet contemplation standing at the wheel, looking across the horizon, keeping an eye on the crew. It was at these times he looked at and admired the two boys, almost men, and thought about his own younger days when he first went to sea with Jack's father.

This was the crew of seven that sailed out of Exmouth in June 1631 aboard the Maid of Sidmouth, heading south-west towards Portugal. The ship was laden with fine cloth made from wool, which was in demand in the Iberian Peninsula and would fetch a good price. Captain Weston and the crew, who would be armed and trained in how to fight with swords and daggers for their security and that of the cargo, would deliver the cargo to a merchant near the harbour. Then with a credit promissary note, not gold or silver for fear of theft, they would purchase Port from another merchant and bring it back to Exmouth. On completion of this contract they would all be well paid, Captain Weston receiving the largest sum, plus they would all receive twenty bottles of fine fortified wine.

The weather was perfect, sunny in the daylight hours and a good wind that blew in their favour. These were conditions that put the crew in good heart; sailing the Maid of Sidmouth could be hard work but clement weather made it more bearable, almost enjoyable as they spent hours singing shanties with individual voices that could never gain a place in their church choirs but together formed a deep powerful harmony. Callum and Jack were novices in all areas, including their knowledge of these songs, but they were eager and quick to learn.

It was always one of the older men that would start a shanty in a raw gravel voice…

"In South Devon I was born, heave away, haul away
In South Devon is my maid, to her I will return, heave away, haul away
Come on boys we will sail, heave away, haul away
Portugal is not far away, heave away, haul away
We'll sell our wool and buy their Port, heave away, haul away
Then return to our maids, heave away, haul away"

Callum and Jack loved the camaraderie of being part of a ship's crew; for the first time in their lives they were not boys but equals, doing the same work as men. There was clearly a hierarchy but because they could match the older men physically they were shown respect. They were intelligent enough to realise that providing they showed the men respect as their elders and listened to instructions they were welcomed into the group. Any initial suspicion the others had of two untrained arrogant pups quickly disappeared after several days at sea, when they could see the two young men would be an asset rather than a liability. In truth, Callum was stronger than everyone else on the ship, which strengthened the status of the boys even more. This could've been a problem for John and Edward, the two men in their twenties, a boy of only eighteen showing off his muscles, whereas the old sea-dogs couldn't really care, they'd seen it all before. However, they were all impressed at the sight of Callum raising the mainsail by himself, a task normally performed by two men.

"Look at the boy," John said to Edward.

"He's got the strength of two men, maybe he will make a useful sailor."

"Yes, and useful in a fight if necessary," Edward replied.

John nodded in agreement, but asked "Are you speaking of a tavern brawl after supping ale, fending off robbers after our cargo on land, or Corsairs?"

Edward looked at his friend, like every sailor in the West Country who went to sea in fear of Barbary pirates, even if they would never openly say so. They'd heard of reports of ships, cargo and crew being taken at sea, particularly away from the coastline where they couldn't make a dash for land and safety. This voyage around the north-west tip of France and down into the Bay of Biscay was particularly fraught with danger and in this year it seemed to be worse than ever.

"Would any of us fight the latter," John added.

They both knew stories of the ferocious brutality displayed by Corsairs. Stories told by the few men who had escaped on a piece of floating wood left behind from a sunken ship, or some who were left to live, cast away in small boats to report what had happened. Old men were of no use to Corsairs; if they resisted boarding by the pirates they were killed, or thrown into the sea to drown for sport, their last sight before submerging for good being mocking Corsairs laughing derisively. Their best hope was to offer no resistance, surrender, show humility and hope they might be sent back to England to spread the reputation and fear of Barbary Corsairs. The option for younger sailors was less hopeful; fight and inevitably die, as they were invariably outnumbered, or surrender and face a life in bondage.

The older members of the crew were fascinated by Callum, the boy with the strength of two men. He was known to have been raised by the women in his family, to which they attributed his quiet manner.

"Why would the boy have a lot to say, he's had to listen to too many words in his short life."

Arthur the old sea-dog sneered, half joking but also half serious. His experience of women had not been happy or successful.

"Is that why your woman left you Arthur?"

Edward quipped, raising laughter from the rest of them.

Arthur flashed him a look that in a tavern could've led to a brawl, but on-board ship at sea was no place to settle a disagreement with a fight, they depended on each other too much.

"Yes, she left me, that be true but she knows if I ever find her I will slit her face from her mouth to her ear, so she can wear a permanent smile."

It was said without humour, suffused with bitter malice, so the laughter stopped abruptly, leaving them all to wonder about Arthur. Callum could not contemplate harming any woman, having known only love and kindness from his mother and grandmother, but he wouldn't say anything to the older man. He just fixed a cold stare and thought about what he'd do to Arthur should he ever make the mistake of harming any women in the Longbow family.

Callum, the maternal grandson of a Scot, was always a tall healthy boy and as he went through adolescence he became stronger, which was enhanced by him working in the fields whenever he could, in an effort to help his mother. With a small piece of land, barely two acres, they could just about grow most of the vegetables they needed, keep two cows, twenty chickens and a cockerel. He didn't know it at the time but Callum's diet was healthy, he breathed fresh air and enjoyed physical work. The result was an eighteen year-old who towered over his peers and most grown men, endowed with strong arms, legs and a powerful chest. Leaving his mother and grandmother wasn't easy but the pull of the sea was irresistible, his mother had tried to dissuade him but, in the end, sent him with her blessing. For her son this first voyage was a dream come true, being a member of a ship's crew, the strongest man in that crew.

"His family name is Longbow, no wonder his arms are like iron. He must be the descendent of one of Henry V's bowmen who won the day against the French at Agincourt."

Harry, the other old sea-dog was speaking. He was of a kinder temperament than Arthur, less likely to make a cruel comment and therefore more likeable. Also, Harry was more like Captain Weston having a fondness for the two boys, admiring their youthful vigour, which reminded him of how he was thirty years before.

Captain Weston was very satisfied with his crew as sailors; they worked hard as individuals but importantly meshed well as a team, which was important on a ship. If one was struggling with a weight or a sail, whoever was close would quickly help. This was more often the case with the two older men, Arthur and Harry, who at their age would always be carried to some extent by their younger, stronger crewmates, but the captain knew they were worth having on the ship for their experience. If he needed to rest, he could rely on them to navigate and it was not uncommon for captains to be taken ill or incapacitated in some way. Arthur, for all his unpleasantness, was also a good cook. However, what Captain Weston didn't know was what his crew of six would be like in a fight. Lots of men could talk a good fight, maybe claiming they'd served in the navy or as soldiers on land. He wouldn't know the truth about them until the situation arose.

The captain decided to organise training with cutlasses and daggers, which the men did for thirty minutes each day. Any longer would've been a hindrance to their work as sailors, as physical combat was fatiguing. The ship could be handled by him and two men if the sea was calm, allowing the other four to train, so each man practised for two thirty minutes sessions in a three-day cycle. They used real weapons with the sharp edges lined with corks saved from bottles when James Weston was ashore.

This was another aspect of being away from home and their mothers that both Callum and Jack enjoyed. Like all boys they'd played at soldiering for hours with their friends, using wooden swords, going at it as if their lives depended on it. Now on board the Maid of Sidmouth they were taking it a step further with real weapons. Captain Weston had brought a selection on the voyage, for protecting the cargo and possibly themselves. The weapons varied in size and weight and there were enough to provide each man with two or three to choose from, appropriate to their size and strength. Callum was flattered to be handed the largest and heaviest, Arthur and Harry were rewarded with the smaller, lighter weapons. There were pikestaffs, long wooden poles with sharp spikes, which all of the men could handle and were used to stop attackers boarding the ship. This was something Captain Weston hoped and prayed they wouldn't need to deploy. A fight on land against robbers was something he didn't savour but was a fight he had some confidence he could win against say up to a dozen attackers. However, like the older members of the crew he dreaded an attack from Barbary Corsairs, particularly as in three decades as a captain he had never heard of a small merchant ship like the 'Maid' fighting off such an onslaught. The best hope they had was to out-run Corsairs with a kind wind and get to the safety of a friendly harbour, or even to just dry land where they could abandon the ship and save themselves. The problem with this latter option was that the Corsairs were also great seamen and their ships were often galleys, which had the option of using oarsman for additional power. If the wind was light this use of human muscle made it virtually impossible to escape from a Corsair galley.

"Dear God, no Corsairs Lord." Weston said each night before sleeping and repeated each morning. In the last twenty years since English ships had started being taken by 'Barbary Bastards', as they were often referred to in the taverns of coastal towns, his prayers had been answered and Captain Weston had developed a reputation as a ship's master who had the seamanship and guile to elude a Barbary galley. However, Weston knew it had been due to good fortune and hoped it would continue for just one or two more voyages.

"One more voyage, please God," was another one of his brief prayers to the Almighty. Escaping two or three Corsair ships was almost impossible sailing across the great expanse of water that was the Bay of Biscay, their only hope being that there might be Spanish warships nearby, keeping the Corsairs at a distance.

"The Spanish hate the Barbary slavers more than anything else, even more than us Protestants. Well at least their soldiers and sailors do, their priests and bishops might disagree."

Captain Weston was explaining to the older men, who could remember the days of the old Queen and the Armada and were still nervous about sailing through Spanish waters. They were all enjoying the warm air under the stars before turning in for the night.

"Aye, that be true Captain. I remember the year our Scottish King signed the treaty with Spain and after decades of war and threat of invasion they've become our friends."

Harry had spoken but Arthur interrupted him.

"That is all well and good mate, but now the heathen Corsairs see us as their hated enemy's friend and we're fair game for enslavement. I think I preferred it before, the risks, the danger and fighting was more straightforward. English and Spanish, sailors and soldiers fighting like honest Christians. Not like these devils, seizing our ships, cargo, men, women and children."

"Aye Arthur, I've heard the markets of Algiers, Salle and Tunis are full of English, Irish, Welsh, Scots and even Scandinavians, Captain…"

Harry said it as much as a question as a statement, interested to hear the captain's view.

"You could be right Harry, we don't know exactly how many from our islands have been taken by these pirates. Parliament seems to keep quiet about it and King James was more concerned about our navy, what was left of it, being sent across the Atlantic. Maybe Parliament is hiding the true numbers from us, to avoid scaring us from sailing and the rich merchants in London not making their fortunes."

"Aye Captain, that be more likely to be closer to the truth." Arthur said in disgust and spat a mouthful of dry biscuit into the sea.

Harry agreed "Aye Captain, that be the truth of it."

"One thing I do know though boys, is that we're not the only ones and we're not the most, not by a long way. We've been suffering badly these last twenty years but those North African Arabic-speaking bastards have been taking captives from Portugal, Spain, Italy, Greece and the Balkans for much longer and the numbers are huge."

"Where do they all go Captain and what do they do?"

Jack asked. He and Callum had been listening quietly, respectfully, but he couldn't remain silent any longer.

"The Ottoman Turks need thousands of new slaves every year Jack. We've been largely spared compared to those Christian countries that have a Mediterranean coastline. Once they're taken to Algiers or one of the other Barbary States, they are sold into a life of hard labour on land building harbours, palaces and mosques. Or if they're unlucky they become galley slaves, chained to an oar for the rest of their days."

Jack's jaw dropped at the prospect and Captain Weston went on.

"They need mainly men for those tasks boys but the few women who are taken are sold as concubines, sex slaves. If they're lucky they will be one of many in a rich Turk's harem. Some might become domestic servants if they're really lucky."

He decided to stop there, as he wanted the boys to know what could happen, but he didn't want to scare them and have a tired crew due to lack of sleep. Callum and Jack got to sleep eventually that night but they both lay awake longer than usual, thinking about what the Captain said.

The voyage of the Maid of Sidmouth across the Bay of Biscay went smoothly, helped by a good north-east wind which took them directly to the north-west corner of the Iberian Peninsula and past the city of Coruna. From there it was a straight forward turn to the south down the coast to the city of Porto.

Captain Weston was happy and relieved as they sailed into Porto and moored. He was even more so once they left after two days, having delivered their cargo to the merchant, who also arranged for their credit note to be exchanged for the Port wine to be taken back to England. No money, gold or silver was required or exchanged. Weston reflected on how civilised this system was and how reassuring it was to see how trade, which was mutually beneficial, could bring nations together.

Furthermore, his crew of six was able to have a break from sea-faring and enjoy the taverns of Porto without any problem. He made it clear that what they got up to he didn't care or need to know, as long as they were ready to sail after two days.

All of them felt good as they sailed out of Porto, each of the six members of the crew had enjoyed the city and what it had to offer visiting seamen. Their feeling of well-being was lifted by the knowledge that their return cargo was a strong wine that they could enjoy or sell once they got their agreed share. Captain Weston knew he had to head directly west out of Porto deep into the Atlantic Ocean for a day or more. Then they should be able to pick up a south-westerly wind that would take them straight towards the south-west corner of England.

Taro

After three days the Maid was approaching the north-west tip of France, not far from the town of Brest, getting closer to the English Channel. 'Just two more days,' Weston thought to himself, looking to the east and the bright sun coming up over France. All of the men were looking in the same direction, towards the sun and home, so none of them were initially aware of three dots on the horizon behind them, coming from the south. If they had seen the dots that quickly grew to take the shape of three ships, they might have taken evasive action sooner by turning east and sailing towards Brest.

"Captain, Captain!"

Arthur was the first to see them and even if they had seen the three ships earlier, it is questionable whether they could've outrun them. They grew in size with each minute and even though Captain Weston turned towards the east to get the full force of the wind into the mainsail, he could see the chasing ships were moving faster. His darkest fear was being realised, he knew they were Corsairs and could begin to see they had the advantage of big mainsails and oars. One ship was much larger than the other two, which were quicker and closing fast.

"Come on boys, we can try to outrun them and get to Brest."

Weston implored his men, knowing it was futile. The French town was not even in sight.

"Shall we fight Captain?" Callum asked .

"No point lad, we seven are no match. Our only hope is to catch a quick wind and get to safety. Once they board the Maid we're at their mercy."

There was no shouting from the seven men on the Maid. They just put every muscle and sinew into sailing her better and faster than they'd ever done before. However, they found the two small Barbary galleys were so fast the chase was soon over. Two small galleys, powered by oarsmen came towards them from behind either side of the Maid and they could clearly hear the calls and shouting in a language they didn't understand. Weston knew from the tone of the voices it would be unwise to continue trying to escape. Surrender might be their best hope of survival.

"Boys, that's enough, stop sailing. It's over. Lower the sail."

With that order the Maid slowed and all they could do was stand and watch the two galleys come alongside. Six men from each of the galleys jumped aboard the Maid, grabbing ropes to help them with one hand, all of them carrying a sabre in the other.

"I'm Captain.."

But before he could say a third word Weston was struck from behind with the handle of a sabre. He fell to the deck and didn't see the next blow with the other more fatal end of the sabre. A long wound opened across his neck and he bled to death in front of Jack.

"Get down, get down infidel!"

Khaled screamed with venom and waved his blood-stained sabre that had ended Captain Weston's life. The six remaining men didn't understand his words but as he pointed down with his free hand they understood. Each man fell to his knees and put their hands over their heads.

The large man who had killed the Captain walked amongst them looking at them intently. Callum didn't want to stare for fear of incurring his anger but couldn't help but notice the look on his face. It only lasted a minute, his inspection of the remaining six members of the crew, then he screamed, which caused them all to look up.

"Infidel!"

Khaled then calmly walked over to Harry and brought his sabre across the old seamen's face and neck. Harry slumped to the deck. He took two steps towards Arthur, who saw what was coming and got to his feet and pleaded for his life.

"I will convert to Islam, please."

However, Khaled didn't understand the words of the Englishman and wasn't likely to change his mind. Arthur raised his arms to protect his head and as he did so Khaled drew his dagger and thrust it into Arthur's stomach pulling it up towards his chest. Arthur's lifeless body joined Weston's and Harry's on the deck of the Maid.

Callum, Edward, Jack and John remained still on their knees with their hands on their heads. They were without weapons surrounded by twelve heavily armed Corsairs, each of them thought this was the end. The leader who had killed the other three shouted commands to the other Corsairs and rope that had been thrown aboard the Maid from the galleys, was used to tie them making escape impossible. The remaining four were hauled to their feet and taken to the side of the Maid and pulled onto the galleys. Callum and the others realised at that point they weren't going to be killed. What Callum also noticed was that the leader who had done the killing was smiling and laughing. He had enjoyed every second of his work on the Maid.

A short time later on board the large galley Said looked at their catch and turned to Khaled.

"Four men, we could've had seven to use in our galleys, or sell in the market."

"The other three were too old Said, and they were unwilling."

Khaled tried to explain with a grin but Said turned away shaking his head. He had observed what had happened and thought about the loss of money due to Khaled's lust for blood.

"Khaled, Khaled my brother, you just destroyed some of our profit. The three older men might not have been as valuable as the younger ones but ten pieces of silver is more than none."

Said paused to think, just ten pieces of silver for the life of a man, thirty pieces of silver they won't have on their return to Algiers.

"Leave those three where they are" Said called. "Don't sink the ship, let it drift to send a message to Christian sailors."

Captain Weston, Arthur and Harry lay dead where they fell on the Maid of Sidmouth.

"I hope the seagulls don't eat them before they receive a Christian burial."

Khaled quipped loudly for the benefit of the other Corsairs and laughed at his own joke.

The four captives sat on the lower deck shackled to great iron links that ran down the middle of the deck. Each one of them was chained to the man in front and behind, as well as the central chain along the deck. Sitting in silence they thought about their three shipmates, who were now no more than food for seagulls or fish in the Bay of Biscay. No-one spoke, the brutality of their captors had already been made evident and if they were not going to join Captain Weston, Arthur and Harry, they would do well to avoid antagonising the huge slave overseer, as well as the one who seemed to be one of the Corsair leaders who despatched the three older members of the Maid of Sidmouth's crew. It was obvious to all four men that this was the initial strategy they must follow if they were to survive.

From where they sat they had a good view of what they expected to be their fate. Three steps to either side of them were two banks of men chained to oars. On each side of the ship were eight oars, two men chained to each oar, making thirty-two oarsmen. Any doubt over whether these men were slaves was quickly settled by the shackles, their faces and the occasional crack of a whip resulting in a cry of pain and blood on a man's back.

'So this is it,' Callum thought. 'This is the life of a galley slave that English seamen sailed in fear of.'

A look at the faces of the other three would've told him they shared his thoughts.

The role of the slave overseer was clearly critical in powering the ship if there was little wind and the oars were employed at the command of the two Corsair leaders on the bridge. This huge man with the whip walked up and down the deck as the slaves rowed bellowing commands, in a language the crew of the Maid did not understand. Whether the slaves were able to understand his language was not known but it was clear the time they'd spent in bondage had enabled them to learn key some commands, their education enhanced by the application of the whip.

"Taro, Taro, we need to get to our destination tonight, not tomorrow, pick it up."

Khaled screamed from the bridge to Taro, who was at the front of the ship standing just behind the men chained to the first two oars. A few of the slaves had enough knowledge of Arabic to know what was coming.

"In time with the front row."

Taro bellowed and beat the drum to set the pace, which the front four oarsmen began to keep. All thirty-two of the slaves moved to a quicker pace in time with the drum but one oar was struggling to keep in time and Taro bore down on it and raised his whip. Both of the men attached to the miscreant oar let out cries of pain as their backs were opened with lines of blood. He raised his whip to administer further instruction but he was stopped by a command from the other Corsair leader.

"Enough Taro, give them time to correct themselves and get in time with the others."

Said's voice was firm and clear, so Taro stopped applying the whip and looked up at his commander with disappointment.

Keeping silent for fear of attracting the attention of the overseer, Callum, Jack, Edward and John had plenty of time to observe the workings of the oarsmen. None of them were old, they were strong and rowed with power. There was some respite for the thirty-two slaves when the wind picked up, the great mainsail was unfurled, the oars were raised and pulled in. Then the Corsair sailors would take over and the slave galley would resemble a normal ship. At this time the slaves would be given water, some food, then slump forward to rest, leaning on the oars to which they remained chained.

It was clear from the sun in the morning that they were heading north towards England. Callum looked around at this large ship that could hold many more slaves; thirty-two slaves were helping to power a ship with only twenty-five corsairs aboard. Also, there were the other two smaller ships that had initially caught and captured the Maid. On board the large galley on which they sat there was a large empty space along the middle of the deck that could clearly accommodate many more than just the four of them. It became clear in his mind that a long voyage for three Barbary slave ships would not be undertaken for the capture of just four men. As Callum realised the coast of England was their likely destination, his heart sank further at the thought of who else might be filling the empty space on the deck of the large galley.

The next day the wind dropped to a speed that barely dented the mainsail and the command went up for the oarsmen. All thirty-two men seemed to understand and the lack of wind had already reminded them of what was required. Taro sprang into action on the command of Khaled, the slaves quickly responding to his shouts and the beat of the drum.

All four of the crew of the Maid watched intently as the machinery of a slave galley operated in unison but after some time of rowing it became clear that one oar was not synchronised. They could all see it was the same one manned by the two men who had received lashes from Taro the previous day. The two men were not old but looked exhausted and weak, in fact they looked ill. Both of them struggled to keep up with the oar in front of them, their faces looked anguished knowing what was coming.

Taro bellowed and his whip cracked in the air before being applied with force. He was frustrated at their inability to keep up and it turned to anger as he set about them.

"Keep up! Keep up pig-eating infidel!"

With that he struck one of the two struggling oarsmen with his club. The slave slumped forward but had the presence of mind to know he had to sit up and row in time if he was to survive. His partner to his side was whipped.

Said and Khaled looked on from the bridge. Khaled smiled, he liked to see Taro in full flow applying discipline and the look of terror on the faces of the recipients provided him with some humour to punctuate the tedium of the voyage. Said had a different perspective. To him each slave was an asset, important in powering the ship and always worth money in the slave market, if they hadn't been half beaten to death or maimed. However, Said also knew he couldn't always intervene to stop the sadism of Khaled and Taro. He needed to keep the two of them satisfied, and if the slaves were not able to keep up it was better to 'lance the boil', removing them from the crew. The other slaves needed to be reminded of what happened if they were no longer an asset but a liability, but unlike Khaled he did not like to see their removal drawn out in a scene of torture. After a short while of allowing Taro to use the two flawed slaves as an example to the rest of the crew, Said decided to be merciful, but he could not appear to be weak or soft.

"Taro, these two useless infidels are slowing us down, remove and dispose of them. Then replace them."

Said shouted with a cold forceful voice, hiding the regret he felt at ordering the death of two slaves who could've been sold at market, but he knew that these displays of ruthlessness were sometimes necessary.

Taro was not disappointed at this command, as it allowed him to display another part of his discipline routine to the other slaves. He calmly walked up behind the two, dropped his whip replacing it with a dagger, then simply opened their throats. The oarsmen behind them closed their eyes for a moment but dare not stop rowing. The two dead men were unchained by the overseer, lifted over the side and dropped into the sea.

The oar of the two oarsmen who were now in a sea grave, had been pulled in by Taro and he looked round for further instruction.

"Taro, get two of them to that oar," Said commanded, nodding towards the four members of the crew of the Maid.

"Taro, use the two younger ones, I want to see if they're worth keeping or selling."

Said had been looking at the four captives and wondering whether they would be worth keeping for his own crew. The two younger ones looked strong, particularly the bigger one.

Taro walked over to Callum and Jack, followed by two Corsairs holding sabres. It was unlikely that two unchained slaves would attempt rebellion, the numbers were insurmountable but there was no point in taking any risks. Sometimes captives could become overcome by grief and a sense of hopelessness, resulting in a frenzied attack on the nearest men who had captured them. Taro wasn't afraid of any infidel slave but as ever Said was concerned about not only his valuable cargo but also the well-being of a vital member of his crew. Taro had his defects but he was crucial in making the ship operate effectively.

They needn't have worried, both Callum and Jack knew that to fight here would be suicidal, even if they were to die taking some corsairs with them. Being submissive was clearly the best choice in this situation so they followed Taro to the unmanned oar and were chained to the bench where the two discarded slaves had sat just a short time before.

Taro shouted at them with menace, words they didn't understand but could guess. Behind them a voice spoke quietly.

"Follow the two men in front of you. Keep in time, when their oar enters the sea so does yours."

Callum didn't look round for fear of drawing the wrath of the overseer but nodded and spoke quietly.

"Thank you."

"Come on infidel, row or follow the other two into the sea."

Their first attempt to row as part of a crew of thirty-two slaves was okay but not good enough, being late their oar banged against the oar behind. The response of the overseer was swift and the two friends were both handed a stroke of his whip, transmitting a searing pain and they both let out a cry as their backs were opened with three lines of blood. Said stood at the bridge observing, wondering whether these two young captives would make it. He'd already decided that if they couldn't master the skill required of a galley slave he wouldn't let Khaled and Taro kill them. They would be chained and sold as quickly as possible in the market for whatever he could get for them.

However, Callum and Jack didn't know Said's plan, nor did Taro and the rest of the crew. The two young Englishmen were reeling from the pain but tried to row in time with the oar in front. As the oars lifted and were pulled forward to enter the sea Callum and Jack joined in, but Jack was feeling the pain from the whip and his hands slipped from the oar and he fell forward on the bench, cracking his jaw against the thick wooden handle he should have been holding. Callum realised the danger immediately, managing to keep control of the oar and somehow kept rowing in time. But that didn't save Jack from what they all knew was coming as Taro walked over whip in one hand, club in the other.

"Tell him to sit up, hold the oar and row," the voice from behind urged.

"Sit up Jack, Jack!"

Callum's plea was not answered by Jack quick enough and as he was clambering back onto the bench he felt another lash from Taro's whip.

"Infidel!" Taro roared "Row or die!"

Jack slumped forward over the oar, making it even harder for Callum to maintain their stroke. Jack was almost useless, like a lame horse at the plough. Callum became more concerned and feared he was about to lose his friend.

"Jack, sit up and hold the oar, please Jack."

Callum knew he could row for them both but his friend had to appear to be helping.

Taro roared with laughter, clearly enjoying the drama in which he was a prominent player, knowing everyone's eyes were on him. He walked over to them again, this time waving the club which would finish off the smaller of the two who wasn't up to scratch. Said was letting the drama go as far as possible before intervening, knowing he had to let Taro have his moment. Just as Taro raised his club Jack managed to sit up and take hold of the oar.

"Wait Taro."

Said shouted loudly and the huge overseer kept his club raised as the English boys joined the stroke in unison with the other thirty oarsmen.

"Come on Jack, we can do this."

Callum didn't look at him, he just kept urging him.

"Stay with me Jack, just sit up and hold on to the oar."

Taro's disappointment was again visible in his face, like a lead actor removed from the stage by the director before the final scene. Jack was able to recover from a state of semi-consciousness and trying to help his friend who had carried and saved him. Khaled and Said had watched the drama intently and looked at each other.

"Maybe these two are worth keeping." Khaled had enjoyed the little drama and was impressed. Said nodded in agreement.

"The big one certainly is."

He liked what he'd seen. More importantly he wasn't going to lose another valuable asset, they would either make it as oarsmen, or he was confident they could fetch a good price.

"Slow the stroke Taro!"

It was clear to Said the big overseer was frustrated by the lost opportunity to display his brutality and was driving the oarsmen hard with a faster beat on the drum. They could see what he was doing, working them hard with the intention of seeing one of them falter. Said looked at Khaled, who was amused by Taro's antics.

"He wants to break them but he doesn't seem to understand they're more valuable to us alive than dead."

Said was sharing his thoughts with his friend and trying to get him to grasp the financial consequences of Taro's discipline.

"Yes, but if you are soft on the slaves they won't respect you Said."

Khaled's philosophy was not much different to Taro's and Said knew that it was something he would always have to keep his eye on. He let Taro continue with his supervision of the slaves at the slower rate but kept an eye on the young Englishman who had struggled. Thankfully after a while a good wind got up, rowing was unnecessary and he could command Taro to bring the oars in, allowing the slaves to rest and the great mainsail provided all the power they needed.

As the tension of the drama subsided and the galleys sailed towards England, Said was left to his thoughts. He loved the life of a Corsair at sea and the excitement of the chase, which usually resulted in the capture of a Christian ship and taking captives. He knew being a slave must be a horrible life and felt some empathy, but he had no qualms about his chosen trade. Slavery and possible capture were a feature of life for everyone sailing the seas, Christian and Muslim alike. What he didn't feel comfortable with was the brutality of Khaled and Taro. He could kill a man but didn't gain any pleasure in torture or cruelty. He'd seen the look in Khaled's eyes many times since that evening when four young men tried to rob them and Khaled killed three of them in the streets of Algiers. Would his friend ever change, he wondered? Always a hard man, Khaled had become more brutal as time passed since the death of Aisha.

"A dead slave is worth nothing Khaled."

Said had told his friend many times.

Laura

Laura's childhood living on a small farm and attending school a few days a week became happy and secure. Leaving childhood behind and going through adolescence, by the time she was fifteen years of age it was clear she was going to be a beautiful woman. "Just like her mother" John would say proudly. Laura's skin was clear and fair, her hair blonde, her eyes as blue as the sky on a sunny day. Naturally she was popular with the other young people in the village, surrounding hamlets and farms. By the time she was sixteen the boys and young men all knew of her as the prettiest girl, drawing admiring glances when she walked through the village. Her older brother and sister had quickly come to love her so by the time she was an adolescent, attracting the attention of boys, they were fiercely protective. James was a strong young man who worked on the farm with his father, and the local lads knew it was unwise to make indiscreet comments about the beautiful Laura. Susan, also an attractive young woman, albeit not the equal of her sister, was aware of the dangers that could exist for a girl so pleasing to the eye of men. She was always watchful and counselled Laura on what she should and shouldn't do, what she should and shouldn't wear.

Mary and John would talk about their three children when they were alone. By 1630 they were conscious that in the next few years there would be changes in their children's lives and their family.

James was increasingly taking on the running of the farm, much to John's pleasure and pride, although he was still to prefix much of what he would say with "Listen lad…." Fortunately, James admired his father and had the modesty to do just that, resulting in them working well together as a team. He would inherit the farm, by which time he would hopefully have a wife and his own children to continue the name of Baddow as respected local farmers.

Susan was eighteen years of age and had a friendship with Edward Miller, a young man two years her elder who lived on a farm just three miles away.

"Edward will be a good match for Susan. He's a hard-working boy from a good family," Mary said.

"Aye, I've always got on well with the Millers, even if I did have a few scraps with his father, William, when we were boys." John said with a smile.

"Oh John, you didn't." Mary was concerned Susan might become embroiled in an old family feud and held John's arm.

"Don't worry, my dear wife. We were about nine years of age and by the time we were eleven we were good friends."

It was only on rare occasions that John thought about his childhood, it was so long ago and his two marriages to two wonderful women had filled his consciousness. He felt blessed that the last two decades had been filled with first Matilda and then Mary. The emotions of two marriages and the devastating loss of Matilda seemed to be all he could remember, his own childhood and adolescence being a distant hazy memory.
He now lived every day working hard but in a happy state, everything being to provide Mary and their three children with safety and security.

The future of Laura, their youngest and still a girl of sixteen, caused them more concern. If she wasn't so beautiful they might have been less worried but they knew she would inevitably draw the attention of men who might not be honourable. They appreciated the protection that James and Susan had provided but feared that as they quite rightly pursued their own courtships, they would not always be able to shield her from advances of good and bad men. Potential danger was always apparent when they went to market and fairs in nearby towns. Everyone knew them in Megavissey, but elsewhere lay peril for a beautiful girl surrounded by men. John was particularly irritated when the sons of wealthy families, sometimes titled, would stare intently at Laura.

"Look at them, they seem to think a beautiful girl from the country is fair game, merely a sport to satisfy their desires."

"It's always been that way John."

Mary was always conscious of her own demise as a young woman at the hands of an older sophisticated man, who didn't stay to do the decent thing.

Despite the fun to be had in the bigger towns, they were always relieved to get home to their farm, where their children, particularly Laura, were safe.

It was the predicament of Laura, her beauty and her honour, that led them to agree that her marriage was more urgent than her older siblings. Still only sixteen and too young to marry but it was an issue that they were increasingly talking about and considering.

"What about that boy, the son of the minister. He's a nice boy and you'd hope he's been raised with good Christian values."

Mary laughed.

"Well at least he's got that."

This conversation was frequently played-out through the spring and summer of 1630, and whilst they could often laugh about it as they considered the suitability of different young men, they were also aware it was a problem that was not going away.

John and Mary weren't to know they weren't the only people who had Laura's future on their minds. Two others thought about it even more than them. Laura had from the age of fourteen admired William Higson, a local boy a year older than her who lived in the village, the son of the teacher.

William had a mutual respect for Laura Baddow. They had come to know each other at the school and it was only once they had left and then saw each other at church on Sundays, as well as occasionally around the village, that as a young man Will became attracted to her and found himself often thinking of her. He would always go out of his way to greet her in a respectful way with a handsome smile.

"Good morning Miss Laura."

Laura found this odd at first as he had never spoken to her in such a formal manner at school. However, she was happy to play along.

"Good day Master William."

Getting beyond this level of conversation was not easy, Will had to be patient but he was encouraged by the warmth of Laura's smile. By the end of 1630 they would stop and talk whenever the opportunity arose, outside church or in passing in the village. Susan had noticed and teased Laura about the handsome Higson boy but she was confident his intentions were honourable so felt no need to tell their parents. She wasn't to know they would have been delighted due to their concerns over Laura and her future.

In the Spring of 1631 when Laura was just a couple of months away from her eighteenth birthday and Will was close to his nineteenth birthday, John and Mary Baddow were visited by Will Higson and the young man revealed to them his love for their daughter. After the initial shock, John and Mary gathered their thoughts and told Will he had their permission to court their daughter, which consisted of walking with her on a Saturday and Sunday, the primary condition being that Susan should always be in view and Laura should always be home before supper. In reality John and Mary were delighted as they knew the Higsons to be a good family, who were not wealthy but were hard-working, self-sufficient and honest. Will was their eldest son and as his wife Laura's future would be safe and secure.

Their courtship was like a dream to Laura and it was agreed by the young couple and their families that they could wed in June. Will would be nineteen and Laura eighteen, which some folk might think young for a respectable girl to wed, but Laura was tall and strong, as well as beautiful. Fears that a girl barely eighteen-year-old might not be ready for the role of a wife and motherhood did not apply to Laura. Mary reassured John that the girl he loved as his own daughter was strong enough to cope with being intimate with a young husband and childbirth, if they were so blessed nine months later.

"She's just a girl," John protested.

"Don't worry John, trust me I know she is strong and ready to be a wife and a mother."

Mary reassured him as she knew from experience, although secretly she did worry and hoped her daughter's experience of no longer being a maid and childbirth would be happier than her own. It could hardly be worse.

The wedding was arranged for the second Saturday in June, early afternoon in the village church. Mary was able to make Laura a dress, that a noblewoman would've been proud of. Mary had made her daughter a beautiful dress pale green in colour, signifying fertility and that she came from a family that was not poor. Only poor girls would wear a white dress and Mary was proud that despite her prospects eighteen years earlier, her daughter was 'respectable'. Everyone in the village was invited and would attend, weddings were an opportunity for everyone to stop working and come together as a community.

Will stood in the church on that sunny day the proudest young man in Cornwall and when Laura came into the church, up the aisle and stood beside him, he looked round to see that the most beautiful young woman in the county would be his wife.

Raid

The three galleys moored in the shadow of a large headland just before sunset. Said had called the captains of the two smaller ships to come to his larger galley and explained how they would carry-out the raid.

"We are not going to sail into the harbour, it is too small, the inhabitants would see us from afar and flee inland, to hide in places we don't know. I don't want to spend two days here searching for what we've come for."

Said and Khaled had been part of land raids before, which unlike boarding ships at sea could be messy. The prey could flee, Corsairs would have to divide into smaller hunting parties, they could find themselves fighting and losing men in skirmishes. Also, Said knew that if some of his men were out of sight and control they could lose discipline, resorting to rape and slaughter. He wanted a swift, clean raid taking what they had come for, no killing and no rape if possible. The latter only delayed them and gave rise to further ill-discipline.

"Mustafa, you will stay here on this ship. Keep the slaves chained and quiet, use force if necessary. At sunrise Khaled and I will take the other two ships as close to shore as possible, landing with thirty men. We know from the chart that there is a small settlement the other side of the headland. We will find it in the morning and attack just after midday. Wait for a short time after midday, until the sun has moved a little way across the sky, then bring the galleys around the headland and moor as close to the harbour as possible. Use the oars and give your commands quietly. By the time you reach the harbour I hope we will have captured and secured our prey. We will load them onto the ships, take what provisions we can use and make our way to our next destination. Is this plan clear?"

Khaled, Mustafa and the other Corsairs had listened carefully and nodded. They liked Said as their leader; he was calm and explained clearly what was required. They understood their orders and retired for the night.

As the sun rose in the east Said and Khaled took the two smaller ships in as close to the shore as they could safely could, leaving a small crew who would control the oarsmen and bring the ships around the headland and into the harbour after midday. Finding a path that led up through the cliffs the thirty-two Corsairs made their way up and over the headland.

From the top of the cliff Said could see to the north the land descending to a river valley and woodland. The other side of the valley the land rose again to green hills and he took a moment to admire the beauty of this country and compared it to what he could remember of Spain. 'England is so green and the climate is much kinder than Spain. This is June and it is like winter in Granada.' After considering the differences between those two Christian Kingdoms, he decided they would drop down into the woods and follow the river as it flowed west. In the woodland they would be less easily seen and he hoped the river would lead them to the settlement. If they could get there without being seen and surprise their prey, there would be less bloodshed and they could be on the galleys and away long before sunset.

Led by Said and brought up at the rear by Khaled, the Corsairs walked along the side of the river silently in single file, five paces apart. This was a nervous time for Said as they weren't certain to come across the settlement, it was a calculated guess, and they had no idea whether there might be English soldiers about. For all they knew there could be a garrison nearby, although Said thought it unlikely as the chart indicated the settlement they were looking for was small, suggesting it would have few trained fighting men.

After walking for a couple of hours an opening in the woodland allowed them to see ahead, and Said was relieved to see the blue of the ocean sitting there, with land curving to the side.

"The bay." Said whispered to himself.

He signalled to the line of men to stop and sit or crouch under the trees. He and Khaled went a little way forward and could then see the houses, which they counted.

"Thirty houses, possibly more." Khaled whispered to his friend.

Said nodded.

"Yes, which suggests there could be thirty to sixty men, who might resist and fight."

They both pondered the odds. There could even be as many as 100 men but how many would, or could, fight. With surprise on their side and confusion among the English, their small force of thirty-two could combat up to sixty and they were confident of winning, but they would rather not suffer any casualties. Boarding a ship in open sea was more straightforward as their overwhelming numbers and reputation for ruthlessness usually resulted in immediate surrender and pleas for mercy.

"Do you think the men in this settlement will fight?" Khaled whispered.

"I don't know, but if we can surprise them there will be less likelihood of them fighting if they don't know our numbers."

Said decided to take two men with him to get a bit closer and a better idea of the numbers, leaving Khaled in charge of the men and well out of sight.

Just above the settlement was a small woodland and from there Said could see and even hear the voices of the people without being seen. He didn't understand the language but there was excitement in their voices, a sense of happiness, even celebration. It soon became clear that people were leaving their homes and making their way to what he knew, from his life in Spain, was a church. Even if the design was slightly different, it was unmistakable as it was the largest and tallest building in the small settlement.

As everyone having left their houses walked into the church, Said briefly wondered what the occasion could be.

"It could be their holy day of prayer."

"Or it could be a funeral, baptism, or wedding."

The cheerful sounds suggested it wasn't a funeral, unless the infidel had no feelings or respect for their dead. They pondered the scene wondering what was happening.

"It must be celebration of a birth or wedding." Said whispered.

Realising this was a golden opportunity he sent for Khaled to bring the others.

Inside the church it had seemed like an eternity to Laura and Will. The minister was very fond of singing and, whether they liked it or not, they and the congregation would sing before he would conclude the marriage ceremony. Then he finally said the words the young couple thought would never arrive.

"You are now man and wife. Will, you may kiss your bride."

As Will followed the instruction of the minister the church, which was packed with villagers and many from the surrounding area, erupted into cheers. All that remained now was for him and Laura to enjoy the celebrations organised by their parents and start life as man and wife. Proud and completely spellbound by Laura's beauty, Will turned and with her arm on his he led her back down the aisle they'd walked up forty minutes earlier. At the doors they paused as two of Will's friends opened them, allowing Will and Laura to lead the congregation out into the sunshine, where they would turn and thank everyone for coming and sharing their happy day.

Said had devised a plan which he hoped would see them seize their prey and incur few casualties. He had seen that there were about 100 people in the church and only thirty-two Corsairs controlling that number would be difficult, resulting in chaos, possible injury and losses to his own men if the inhabitants fought back. The men they desired for the markets back in Algiers might even escape.

They would wait behind the church, out of sight and when the people began to leave they would take them by surprise, come round to the front and close the doors, which would be secured with chains and shackles. At the same time the door at the back would be locked in the same way. Hopefully only about twenty of the inhabitants would be outside the church, they could secure them with ropes, chains and shackles and decide who to take down to the harbour, where they should find the two small galleys waiting. Said was reasonably confident and knew the critical moment would be when they rushed round from the back of the church as the Christians were leaving, at which point there would be chaos.

Will and Laura walked out through the doors into bright sunshine followed by the maids of honour, the two families and a respectful congregation. The sun was so bright most of them were shielding their eyes with their hands. At the same time fifteen Corsairs crept along the outside walls either side of the church. As twenty or so people filed slowly out through the doors the attack was launched.

There was no shouting by the Corsairs and the wedding party was taken completely by surprise. As twenty-four Corsairs fanned out forming a semi-circle that surrounded the group that was outside the church, the other eight Corsairs moved behind, with clubs and sabres pushing any of the congregation in the doorway back into the church. They closed the doors, securing them with chains and shackles. It wasn't the case that no-one tried to fight but that they were taken completely by surprise. A few men in the doorway tried to push back but they were unarmed and had to step back from the sabre waving Corsairs. Several men received deep cuts to their arms and legs causing those who might fight to retreat back into the church. In the initial panic those inside the church felt relief as the doors were locked.

Those outside were a mixture of men, women and children. Unarmed the men had no chance against the heavily armed Corsairs but instinctively stood in front of their women and children.

For a few moments there a silent stand-off, the two groups facing each other, waiting for the other to move. Will, his father and John Baddow stood at the front of the wedding party, shielding Laura, the other women and a few children from these dark-skinned invaders. Some of the children began to cry and the women held them close, burying their small faces in their dresses so they wouldn't see the horror they feared might happen next, but no slaughter occurred.

"Stay calm everyone, if they wanted to kill us it would have started by now."

As Baddow spoke those words one of the attackers stepped forward, just five steps from them and spoke in a language they didn't understand and was waving his sabre.

"Get down to your knees infidel."

Khaled was gesturing with his sabre but the Christians weren't responding, so he gestured to one of the largest Corsairs at the side. Abdul walked up and struck John Baddow with a large club about the head and as he cried out in pain another blow behind his legs sent him to the ground.

"Get down, get down."

Khaled screamed at them and pointed at John using him as an example.

Mary screamed.

"John!"

She rushed to help her stricken husband but she too was struck about the head and fell to the ground. Panic spread through the crowd of captives and they could hear calling from inside the church but those inside couldn't help them. Will was unsure what to do, fighting seemed futile against these men but what were they going to do, and he feared for Laura.

The Corsairs held their line and stared with menace as Khaled kept screaming.

"Get down infidel, down on your knees."

As he did so the six men who had secured the church door moved behind the captives and started shoving them to the ground. The rest of them got the message and sank to their knees and knew they were completely at the mercy of these men. All of the children and some of the women were crying but Laura was too concerned about her mother and father who had been hurt.

Said signalled to twelve of the men to tie and shackle the captives. He wanted to get this done quickly and get out, which involved him assessing which of the captives would be worth taking down to the galleys. In his mind he had ten men and maybe three women as a good catch for the day. The twenty or so captives were quickly bound and separated into men, women and children. Separating the children from the women caused hysteria amongst the women, crying from the children and shouting from the men. They weren't to know that Said wasn't interested in children but their worse fear was that the children would be taken.

There were five children, eight women and eleven men, including the man and woman who lay on the ground. Said would've liked more men to choose from but he was not about to open the doors of the church, in which the other eighty or so were held. Those inside had stopped pounding on the doors as it was futile but continued to call out to their friends and family held captive the other side of the doors.

"John, Will, what is happening out there?"

Those outside could hear but no-one was willing to answer for fear of the consequence.

Said was weighing up which of the men would make a galley slave and thought about eight of the them, plus the slightly older man who had been struck down by Abdul, if he recovered. Meanwhile Khaled moved amongst the women, holding just a dagger and got pleasure by touching their hair as he held the dagger to their necks or breasts. His menacing pleasure at touching the Christian women as they kneeled on the ground was increased by the fear in their faces and the tears in their eyes.

"Khaled! That's not helping, I want to get what we've come for and get out."

Worse, Khaled's actions were causing panic amongst the captives and excitement amongst the Corsairs. Said did not want rape and slaughter but knew that could be the result of Khaled's actions.

Khaled had moved along the line of women and stopped at Laura.

"This one is the most beautiful, it was her wedding day. Do you think she is a maid?"

Khaled was becoming overcome with lust but Laura could only freeze in terror as he held his dagger to her throat and placed his hand down into her dress, holding her breast.

"Khaled, that's enough!"

Said commanded but that didn't stop him, instead a rock struck him on the head, causing him to drop his dagger and fall away from the girl. John Baddow had got to his feet and had sprung to save his daughter but as he bore down on Khaled the Corsair drew his sabre and brought it across the face and neck of John Baddow, who fell to the ground with a gaping wound, from which his blood poured.

"Father!"

Laura's anguished cry pierced the air. Khaled sneered but he wasn't finished and turned back to Laura.

"That's enough Khaled." Said shouted. "I want that one for the market and she will fetch a higher price if she is a virgin."

This stopped Khaled's advance on Laura but his lust for a woman was still high and he wasn't satisfied, so he turned to the other women.

"This one is spoilt goods now, she's injured and too old to sell as a concubine, but she is pleasing on the eye. She will do."

Khaled pulled Mary to her feet and dragged her out of the line, pulling at her clothes to reveal her arms and part of her breast. As he started to drag her towards a building she was able to bend down and pick up the dagger Khaled had dropped. Unstable on her feet Mary screamed.

"No!"

She lashed out at Khaled, but it wasn't a clean strike and caught him across the arm. However, it did cause him pain and he let go of Mary, but with his good arm he drew his sabre once more. His lust for flesh turned to anger and now he wanted blood. Despite the pain in his other arm he brought the sabre across Mary's legs, causing her to collapse to the ground. Kneeling she was in tears and frantically waved the dagger at Khaled but he simply stepped to the side, raised his sabre above his head and brought it through a wide arc that ended with it buried into her neck. Her head wasn't severed but death must have been quick and Mary's body slumped to the ground.

The slaughter didn't stop there as Will had looked on in silence and anguish up until this point, but then snapped and ran forward towards Khaled. As his charge almost reached its target, a smile appeared on Khaled's face and he side-stepped Will and brought his sabre across the back of Wills left leg, causing him to fall. Unable to stand on both legs due to tendons behind his left knee being severed, he was kneeling as Khaled thrust a dagger into his throat.

For a moment there was silence again, amongst the Corsairs and the Christians. Khaled had been satisfied and walked away. Laura couldn't speak or cry, she just stared at her beloved parents and Will, all killed by a monster in what seemed like a few moments. The young bride was thrown into a state of shock, just ten minutes earlier she was in the church being wed to Will, now her life was destroyed, the three people she loved most were dead.

The selection of the captives to be taken to the galleys was completed and they were led down to the harbour, where the two smaller galleys were waiting. All of this was done with a surprising lack of noise or fuss. The Mevagissey captives were silenced by the brutality they had witnessed and were resigned to their fate.

Despite the violence and the killing of two men who could have been valuable galley slaves, either on one of his ships or for sale in Algiers, Said was grateful it hadn't been worse and was satisfied with his haul of nine men and three women. They were loaded onto the two small galleys along with plenty of food that had been found, food that had been prepared for the wedding celebration. Said looked back at Megavissey from the bridge of one of the galleys and looked at Khaled as he dressed his wound. He would talk to him later as knew it was pointless now.

Laura had risen that morning a young maid looking forward to marriage and a secure life with Will. As the sun went down it had been the worst possible day of her life. She was still a maid but was in chains, her parents and husband slaughtered. Her life and the world could never be the same again. Unlike the other two young women, no tears fell, her emotions were frozen and she simply stared at the deck to which she was shackled.

Baltimore

Said was beginning to feel pleased with the voyage as they sailed west from Megavissey and looked at his fourteen captives chained down the middle of the main deck. Plus the two who had been added to the crew for the oars. However, his ship still had space for six to eight more and the two other galleys could take eight to ten slaves each. Twenty to twenty-five more slaves would make it a very profitable voyage.

At the same time as Said was thinking about the capacity of the three galleys someone else was having similar thoughts but from a different perspective. Callum and Jack had been able to talk during the raid on Megavissey. Taro had been distracted from keeping a close eye on the galley slaves, as he stood at one end of the ship straining to see events unfold in the village. The slaves were all chained anyway, if they called-out they knew they'd face his wrath and there was no Said to stop him. Callum and Jack found they could whisper to each other and the slaves in front and behind. In the time they sat waiting, which was not long, they learned a lot about the hierarchy on the galley, importantly that the tall one Khaled seemed to defer to the quieter, less brutal one called Said. Just behind them sat Pedro, a Portuguese who could speak some Arabic but understood more.

"Where are we heading?" Jack asked quietly.

"Algiers, eventually." Pedro replied, then added.

"But look at the space and chains on the main deck. The other two galleys also have space and chains that need to be used. Most Corsair captives are small numbers of crew and passengers taken from ships at sea. This is unusual, three galleys."

Another voice, this time with an English accent added.

"Aye, this is part of a bigger slaving expedition. Mark my words."

The discussion was interrupted by the return of the Corsairs with twelve captives, nine young or mature men and three young women. Two of the young women were crying and turning to look back at the world they were leaving behind. The third young woman was silent, in a state of shock, stared ahead and seemed to not see or care about what was happening around her. Furthermore, she stood out as she was beautiful, with long blonde hair and wearing a beautiful pale green dress, soiled with dirt.

'Dear God, was this her wedding day?' Callum thought to himself. No wonder she is in shock.

The twelve captives were secured to the great metal bar and all but Laura looked back to Megavissey as the ship sailed west. She felt nothing and was emotionally torn to shreds.

Although Callum might have been wondering similar thoughts as Said about the capacity of the three galleys, what he couldn't know was that Said knew where they were going and that he expected to fill all three galleys with valuable cargo.

Back in Algiers Said had agreed to join a raid on the south coast of Ireland. He did not know this land but the raid was organised and led by a man called Murat Reis, who knew the seas surrounding the islands of Britain and Ireland. What was strange to Said and Khaled was that Murat was not a Berber, Morisco or Ottoman. He was as white as any of the Christian slaves as he came from the land of the Dutch. His name was originally Jan Janszoon Van Harlem but joined the Corsairs and converted to Islam some years earlier.

Murat Reis was a great sea-faring captain, like many Dutchmen, and quickly became an effective and respected Corsair captain. His plan was to raid a town or village on the south coast of Ireland, places that were often remote and not fortified. With a large force of galleys, say six or eight, he believed they could empty a village or small town and come away with more than 100, or even 200 slaves. The potential to capture and sell as many slaves in one raid as they might in months at sea was very attractive. Murat persuaded several Corsair captains of the viability and potential profit of his plan, so along with two other captains, Said had agreed to join Murat in his project. This wasn't a difficult decision to make as Murat Reis had achieved legendary status amongst everyone along the Barbary Coast, even in Istanbul.

"Is it true?" Khaled asked a few weeks earlier. "The great Murat Reis has asked us to join him."

Said had no problem in persuading Khaled, they both knew about the raids led by the Dutchman four years earlier.

"Said, he and the other galleys came back with more than 400 captives from Iceland. Some say it was more than 600." Khaled was laughing as he spoke.

"Yes Khaled, the other captains weren't sure about sailing so far north, where the sea is bitterly cold, but they returned happy."

"The women were all fair in complexion, with golden hair and blue eyes Said. Many were taken straight to the Sultan's Topkapi Palace. They say Murat Reis is the Sultan's favourite Corsair and he paid generously for the girls he was pleased to receive."

Khaled was almost beside himself, thinking about the gold and silver, as well as the women he could've experienced.

"This is a great opportunity for us Khaled." As usual Said wasn't thinking about the women, his eye was on the economic potential. "We could become famous Khaled, the Sultan will be made aware of us and in years to come we will be talked about just as Murat Reis is today."

Three weeks on they were making their way to a rendezvous with the famous Dutchman. It was almost mid-summer and using a chart Murat provided for each of the captains, Said agreed to meet the small fleet of eight ships on the next full moon in the bay of Cape Clear Island. This little island lay at the very south of Ireland, about two days sailing from the south-west tip of England.

Said's three ships sailed west along the coast of England and as they passed the point the English called Land's End they changed direction north-west towards the south coast of Ireland. All of the captives and slave oarsmen could sense something else was going to happen, the position of the sun told them they weren't heading south towards North Africa.

The chart Murat had provided was excellent and Said explained to Khaled how important this was. Sailing around the Mediterranean was easy, every Corsair knew the headlands and islands that made navigation straightforward, but the open seas beyond Gibraltar required more skill.

"Dutch seamen are famous for being great navigators Khaled. Like the Spanish, Portuguese, English and French, they sail across the Atlantic to the Americas to become rich. They even sail around Africa to the East and the land of oriental men. Murat has all the knowledge of the art of navigation, which his people are famous for."

Khaled was totally convinced, he trusted his friend and brother. Their relationship had come a long way since he'd met the nine year-old Morisco years ago in Algiers. As they sailed north-west, towards a town or village that would make them rich, he thought about how they had changed. He was still bigger and stronger but he was happy to allow Said to lead. He let Said make the decisions, he accepted he was wiser and understood the workings of commerce. They made a good team.

Said studied the chart and sure enough on the second evening after leaving the village the coastline of Ireland appeared. They got closer and then sailed west following the coastline until they came across an island that could be the one on the chart. As it got dark the moon appeared and Said could see it was almost full, maybe just a day away. They moored the galleys in a small bay with no signs of houses or people and waited for the morning.

Callum couldn't take his eyes off the girl in the pale green dress, drawn not just by her beauty but also the sadness in her face. She seemed to be devoid of emotions, unaware of what was happening.

"What has she been through and where will she end up?" Jack asked the question in a whisper. He could see his friend was thinking the same thing. They were both saddened as they had a good idea of her fate and they were helpless, unable to save her.

In the morning Said sent one of the smaller galleys to look for the large bay, which was where Murat would be if this was Cape Clear Island. Using just oars, the smallest galley was quick and manoeuvrable, while the rest of them would sit and wait. After a short time of waiting the small galley returned, came alongside and gave them the news they wanted; Murat was there with three galleys, having arrived two days earlier.

Said met with Murat and two other captains aboard Murat's great galley, in a large sheltered bay. The bay faced southwards out to the Atlantic Ocean so they could've stayed there for the rest of the summer and not been seen. However, their stay wouldn't be that long as Murat had a plan. Charts of the south coast of Ireland showed there were a number of towns and villages nearby but the problem was knowing how many people there would be and was there likely to be a garrison or military force. To that end Murat had good fortune as he had approached Cape Clear Island two days earlier.

A fishing vessel was seized and its crew taken captive. The crew of four was young, strong and immediately put in chains, with the exception of the captain, an older man who wouldn't be much use as a galley slave, or fetch much of a price back in Algiers. Fortunately for the old man it was Murat and not Khaled who captured him, and the shrewd Dutchmen saw that the old captain could be of use.

When the old Irishman was brought before the captains he clearly knew he was of no use as a slave and expected to not see another day. He was forlorn, trembling with fear. Like many of his countrymen, Murat could speak several languages and addressed the old man.

"Stop trembling old man. If we wanted to kill you, you would be dead by now."

The old captain looked up.

"Yes Sir. Thank you, Sir."

"We will let you go free old man, providing you help us."

"Yes Sir. Thank you, Sir. I will Sir."

That was it, a bit of good fortune in seizing a local fishing boat and Murat's force had all the information they needed. Without too much squeezing the old man told them about all the nearby villages and towns, how to reach them and what military force there might be.

The closest village was probably the best option, a place called Baltimore, with a population of 200-300. Why stay too long and increase the chance of drawing attention from English men of war. The only reservation was that Baltimore had a small castle.

"Don't deceive us old man. If there's a strong military presence and we lose men, I will make sure your death is slow and painful."

The old man was visibly scared but assured them that it was a small castle, maybe 400 years-old and couldn't hold more that fifteen to twenty men. Murat weighed up the risk and was happy that 100 Corsairs would cause so much havoc that fifteen soldiers would stay inside their old castle for safety, rather than come out and fight.

"And if they want to come out and fight we will make an example of them that will spread terror throughout Ireland." Murat said reassuringly to the other captains, drawing smiles and nodding heads of agreement.

Murat was particularly pleased that Said had made it to the rendezvous. He liked the young Morisco, as brave Corsairs were plentiful but those also blessed with intelligence were far fewer. Furthermore, through his connections with powerful merchants, Said came with three galleys. One large one, like Murat's own huge galley, but also with two smaller, much quicker vessels, like the other two captains who joined his enterprise. This gave Murat a small fleet of two large galleys and four small ones, which would be much better for a smash and grab raid. The two large galleys would moor out of sight, leaving the four smaller ships to sail into the harbour quickly, hopefully returning with 100 or more captives.

There was no reason to wait, they would carry-out the raid the next morning after dawn. The only preparation required was to transfer all of the captives they had already onto the two large galleys. Two overseers and twelve corsairs were enough to leave behind to guard the oarsmen and captives, all of whom would remain chained and shackled.

The four small fast galleys, each powered by thirty-two oarsmen and each carrying twenty-five Corsairs, would be a frightening prospect for a village or small town. Murat was like Said, he wanted the raid to be swift, get in, get the captives and get out. He wasn't interested in rape and killing, for him it was business. Despite the old man's words, he was also a little nervous about the castle. He needn't have worried.

Mary

Mary McGannon looked up at the sky and smiled. It was June 20th, a beautiful summer day and she was in Baltimore for the weekly market. She and her brother Patrick were there as they always were, selling mutton and pork for their father Gerard. The old man loved to farm but was tired of all the fuss at the market, too many whining customers trying to persuade him to lower his price.

"Come on Gerard McGannon, you're no better than a thief, or worse, bloody English Puritans."

Gerard was not greedy, his prices were fair and he invariably lowered them if demand was not high, but he was getting tired of all the wrangling and horse-trading over a fine piece of Irish meat. Fortunately, Patrick and Mary were more than happy to take the meat in to Baltimore to sell. He trusted them and knew they would do a good job of selling it.

"Why not, the farm will be Patrick's soon enough. As long as he doesn't spend all the money in Murphy's Tavern."

"That's right and he'll have Mary there to keep an eye on him."

Gerard had the same conversation with his wife Margaret several times, and each time he got the same reply.

Patrick was a typical farmer's son, big and strong, and sure enough as the eldest son, the farm would one day be his, whereas Mary, whilst being useful around the farm, was different and would rather not marry a farmer. This young woman of twenty-two years loved to go into the village, as well as the larger surrounding towns, enjoying the busy nature of the markets. She knew her parents wanted her to meet someone suitable and from their cart-come-market stall she could survey the comings and goings on this busiest day of the week in Baltimore. Sure, there a few young men that Mary had her eye on but none of them were farmers' sons.

Mary was tall and strong, not thin and weak like some of the town girls. She had a natural beauty about her, with long dark hair, almost black in colour, green eyes and an alluring smile. Certainly, she was admired by many young men, it was a matter of choosing the right one and this young Irish woman was not going to be rushed. 'Sure enough', she thought to herself, 'I'll marry when I'm ready and to who I like'.

Baltimore market was busy that day with stallholders, the local townsfolk and visitors from the surrounding area. Murphy's Tavern was full of men enjoying their beer and the music played by a couple of fiddlers. All of this worked in Murat's favour as the four small galleys came into the harbour quickly. They had been spotted by some young boys playing by the water but no adults were along the dockside, it seemed the whole town was either at the market two roads back and out of sight of the harbour, or in Murphy's Tavern alongside the market.

The young boys who saw the four ships coming into the quayside cheered at first, as the arrival of ships had always been the cause of excitement in the town. Only when it was clear the men who disembarked were not like anyone they'd seen before in their short lives did they begin to become a bit concerned. By then it was too late and even though they did eventually turn and run towards the market place, they were quickly followed by almost 100 Corsairs.

Murat had thoroughly briefed Said, Khaled and the other two captains. He wanted them to spread out through the streets of the town, each of them with fifteen to twenty men, leaving twenty more men to guard their ships in the harbour. The five raiding units would move through the town seizing men and women, mainly men, strong young ones preferably. He made it clear that they were to kill anyone who resisted but they were not to dwell, so each leader had to maintain the discipline of his men. With any luck they could be back at the harbour before any armed resistance could be organised and if soldiers emerged from the castle they would deal with them as a united force.

The five units moved quickly and the first any of the adults in Baltimore knew of the Corsairs was when three of the units came into the market square from three different side streets. Chaos erupted amongst the people in the market, screaming and shouting as panic set in. Some escaped but most were surrounded by forty or more frightening, heavily armed Corsairs. A few men picked up anything that might serve as a weapon and attempted to fight but they had no chance against sabres and clubs. Dealt with swiftly by the more skilled fighters, they died where they fell. Seeing this quick and brutal treatment of resistance the enclosed crowd froze and stood still, allowing the Corsairs to begin tying and chaining those their leaders chose for captivity.

At the same time the other two Corsair units had descended on Murphy's Tavern, where the revellers were initially oblivious to what was happening in the market place. When the alarm was raised amongst the men inside the tavern, their mood turned to a beer-fuelled anger and they pushed each other as they squeezed to get through the door and out into the road to fight. Picking up chairs, tables and anything else they charged at the thirty or so Corsairs, but just as in the market place, this was an unequal fight. Within two minutes twenty or more Irishmen lay dying in the road and the Corsairs hadn't suffered one casualty. Those Irishmen still standing found they sobered up quickly and crowded back into the tavern, bolting the door behind them. Thirteen of the live Irishmen didn't get back into the tavern before the door was bolted and they were quickly seized and shackled, beaten into submission with clubs.

Within two hours of landing Murat's Corsairs had secured over 100 captives. The brutal ferocity of the raid had been witnessed by two soldiers in the tavern, who managed to escape and raced back to the castle. Their account and exaggeration of Corsair numbers persuaded the officer in charge to lock the gates, keeping himself and twelve soldiers safe. They were able to observe the remainder of the proceedings from the castle wall.

Murat and Said went through the lines of captives held in the market place. Mary and Patrick were separated and put in different lines but tried to keep sight of each other, Mary straining her neck to see where her brother was. Word of the slaughter was soon whispered between the captives and Patrick knew putting up any kind of resistance was futile. Looking at the crazed, blood-covered faces of some of the Corsairs, he also realised showing humility was more likely to keep him and Mary alive. Knowing her hot temper, he hoped she would realise this as well. Fortunately, Mary was no fool and word of the killing and the faces of the Corsairs helped her decide to keep her head down, facing the ground.

Said looked round and saw Khaled laughing with some of his unit. Predictably Khaled was at the centre of the fight and killing outside the tavern but there was nothing to chastise him for as the Irishmen had foolishly attacked, instead of surrendering.

Murat had offered Said up to forty of the 120 captives, which was generous but Said agreed a deal which was accepted by Murat. In his mind Said had decided that he would take only young, strong and beautiful captives. Khaled was surprised when it was first shared as an idea but he could see what his friend was trying to do. In Algiers different Corsair leaders and slave traders had different reputations for the quality of their 'product'. Said had persuaded Khaled that their Bagno should become famous throughout Algiers, and eventually throughout the Ottoman Empire, for having the best quality slaves. This would lead to them being sought-out by slave buyers, maybe even the Sultan's Pasha would come to them first when visiting Algiers. So it was that Said agreed with Murat that he would take only twenty to twenty-five of the Baltimore captives, but he would have first choice of the best.

Patrick and Mary found themselves in the first line of captives who were led down to the harbour and loaded onto the first ship, accompanied by Said, Khaled and fifteen Corsairs. Then Murat and the other two captains brought their prizes to the harbour and loaded them onto the other three ships. Within barely three hours Baltimore was robbed of over 100 of its inhabitants and the four small galleys made their way back to the rendezvous with the two larger galleys.

On Said's main galley Mary was chained to the great metal bar alongside Laura but that first afternoon and evening as they sailed south she had been looking back along the deck towards the group of men that contained her brother. Her thoughts weren't about what might happen to herself, she was worried for Patrick after witnessing the brutality and killing of the men in Baltimore.

Eventually as the sun disappeared over the western horizon and it got dark, Mary was overcome with tiredness and lay down alongside the younger woman, who was no more than a girl. Before the light had gone completely and she pulled an old blanket over her to keep warm, Mary looked at the face of Laura. All she could see in the eyes of this beautiful girl was emptiness, with no sign of emotion. Then it was dark and Mary could hear the movement of the galley through the water, as well as the groans and quiet sobbing from some of the other captives. She and Patrick were alive, somehow, they had to stay together. Mary realised there was nothing she could do right there and then, so she closed her eyes and slept.

As the sun appeared in the east Mary was awake and sat up next to the young woman she'd looked at the night before. Laura was also awake and sitting up but didn't look at Mary or acknowledge her in any way. They were sitting apart from the others, on a slightly shaded part of the deck. Unlike the others, the young woman Mary found herself sitting alongside was in a pale green dress, which now torn and dirty, was originally a beautiful garment. The neckline was torn so that having once modestly been just below her neck, was now lower, revealing the top of her breast. At the bottom of the dress the hemline had been torn or cut so it was at her knees. What must have been the bottom part of the dress was now used as a shawl or cover for the girl's head. Despite the trauma of her own capture and her concern for Patrick, Mary was intrigued by the young woman and guessed what might have happened. 'Dear God, she looks like she's been taken captive on her wedding day. Surely that can't be,' Mary thought to herself.

Three days earlier as they had left the coast of Cornwall and sailed towards Ireland, Said had been looking at his prize so far and thinking about how many they might have in total on their return to Algiers. Like Khaled he was struck by the beauty of the fair skinned girl with golden hair. But unlike Khaled he was not filled with lust, rather he was thinking about her value in the market. 'This one is truly beautiful and as it was her wedding day she is probably still a virgin. Maybe the Algiers market is not the place for her, I think the Sultan himself would be interested.' Said was thinking about how he could get word of her to people like Pashas and Viziers, who might have access to the Sultan. Then as he glanced towards the south and the bright sun he had a thought that brought him back to the reality of the moment.

"Taro! Come here."

The big overseer looked up and walked the length of the deck to his master. All of the crew and the captives, with the exception of Laura, looked towards the master at one end of the ship. Everyone was use to the other master barking orders but this one rarely raised his voice. They couldn't hear the conversation between Said and Taro but the captives feared the worse as the overseer drew his dagger, turned and walked towards the captives. He walked pass the men and stopped at the young woman, who was shackled by the main mast and slightly sheltered from the sun. Standing over Laura he spoke in a language she didn't understand.

"Get up, infidel bitch."

Laura sat motionless, still in a state of shock, she could hear his voice but she didn't know what he was saying and didn't care, instead she just stared at the deck. Death right there might come as a relief from the nightmare. Taro grabbed her hair and pulled her to her feet and as he did so two Corsairs stepped behind Laura taking hold of her arms. Standing close to her he held his dagger to her face and grinned. Laura could smell him, feel his foul breath and see his stained teeth. Once again, he was enjoying being centre stage but was curious that the girl showed no fear, no emotion, just the blank look of someone who knew execution was coming, which would be a release from this world.

Callum looked at the spectacle unfolding and wondered what the master had ordered. He wanted to defend the girl but there was nothing he could do or say.

As Taro stood close to the girl's face, whispering what he would like to do to her, the tension amongst the captives was almost tangible. Amongst the crew there was some laughter at the drama that was breaking the boredom of the day's sailing, along with a couple of encouraging calls.

"Go on Taro, show her what you've got."

"Haha, look she's not scared of you fat man!"

That was all the encouragement Taro needed and as Laura's arms were held tight he slowly ran the blade of his dagger down her breast and then down her stomach. However, much to his disappointment the girl continued to show no fear, nothing, she didn't even struggle, just stared out to sea.

"Taro! Thank you for the entertainment. Now do what I asked of you so we can get back to sailing the ship. If I have to come down there and do it myself, you will be sorry. Hurry up!"

Said had watched like everyone else but unlike the rest of the crew he was not amused. He too was intrigued by the reaction, or lack of it, from the girl. However, it was time to get on with sailing to Ireland and Taro's little show was beginning to become an irritating distraction.

The overseer knelt down in front of the girl, held the bottom of the dress taut and cut the material away at her knees. It took a minute, Laura stood motionless making it easier, and the result was a piece of material that was draped over her head. She was pushed down and left alone. Said nodded his approval to Taro and turned to Khaled, who had been watching with interest.

"There, you see, we will protect her from the sun and keep her skin fair. They say the Sultan loves young women with ivory skin, golden hair and blue eyes."

Khaled smiled, he knew Said was right.

Three days later Mary was sitting next to the expressionless girl. The tall attractive young Irish woman reached out and held the other's hand. "Hello, I'm Mary." Laura was still physically numb; her mind had been blank since Mevagissey but she was able to acknowledge the gesture and replied "Thank you."

The ships sailed south and Laura's mind began to fill with thoughts seven days after being taken captive. For a week she had felt and thought nothing but now she started to think about what was happening to her. Her family and Will were constantly in her mind but she was coming to terms with the reality that they were gone. She was alive and owed it to them and herself that she had to survive. For three to four years she had been aware of admiring beauty from boys and young men. Her family had gradually educated her to realise she would be desired by men because of her beauty. She had been as relieved as her parents when her engagement to Will was announced, finally she would be secure and safe from amorous men. Now Laura knew that her parents' worse fears were going to be realised tenfold. Without speaking Laura thought about her future, she sensed her captors didn't intend to kill her, the improvised cover for her head suggested they wanted to look after her. Laura resolved that despite what men might think and do to her, she would not be defined by her beauty, she would be strong. She was still unable to smile or show emotion but one week after Mevagissey her mind was coming alive and she started to think.

Algiers

In Algiers there was great excitement as the five galleys sailed into the harbour. Word had been sent once they had turned south around the headland and approached the great bay. Whispers turned to rumours that spread quickly through the town and the talk everywhere was that Murat and his partners were returning with 100, 200, maybe 300 slaves. This was great news for everyone, as their sale to Ottoman and any other buyers would be good for commerce and benefit the whole city, as gold and silver spent on slaves would trickle down through the economy of the Algiers. There was also the entertainment to be had from seeing the slaves and their faces as they realised their fate.

The harbour was packed with hundreds, maybe a thousand spectators as the five galleys docked and their cargo unloaded. Murat's galley was first, as it was the largest and he was the leader of the whole enterprise, and his eighty-five captives and forty oarsmen filed off his ship tied and chained. They were led through the jeering and laughing crowd, closely guarded by his Corsairs, who were not about to allow any escape at this stage. Nor were they going to let anyone be stolen or molested.

As the line filed through the crowd it was a favourite sport of some men to taunt any women captives with words they couldn't understand but could guess the meaning, particularly if the men could reach them with pinches or even touching their breasts. The screams of the unfortunate young women meant their torment didn't go any further, as the Corsairs guards would quickly turn on the molesters with the pommel of their sabres or club.

After Murat's captives were led away, they were followed through the crowd by Said and Khaled proudly leading their sixty-five, which consisted of their oarsmen and the captives taken on this voyage. The sight of Laura and Mary tied together caused a lot of excitement amongst the crowd of men. Laura with her blonde hair and blue eyes, Mary with her black hair and green eyes, were as beautiful and alluring as any men in Algiers had ever seen. The temptation to touch them was too much for some of the men in the crowd and one rushed forward to feel the flesh of Laura. However, this had been anticipated by Khaled and as the unfortunate young man got to her he was felled by a heavy blow to the back of his head.

"Get back, street dog. If she's anyone's, she's mine!"

Khaled's reputation for brutality was known throughout the city and the closing crowd stepped back. Laura didn't know what he was saying and didn't want any help from the man who a week earlier had killed the three people she loved most. As he stroked her hair and said something else she didn't understand, she felt a shudder at the thought of what his intentions were. Laura was beginning to come out of the state of shock she'd been in for days after Mevagissey, encouraged by the words and kindness of Mary, she even ate some food. Now she found herself in captivity in a foreign land, she had a good idea of what fate lay ahead and she was scared. The warmth shown to her by Mary was all she had to hang on to at the moment, but as they walked through the crowds she wondered how long would that last.

Callum looked on, helpless to do anything but observing everything, noting Laura's torment and the look on Khaled's face. Despite the dark uncertainty of his own fate, he was concerned for this girl he did not know.

Khaled led their sixty-five slaves into the city and through the narrow streets. As they got away from the crowds that had gathered in the harbour the atmosphere eased, with Said at the rear and ten Corsairs they could easily guard and protect their property. Placing Khaled at the front also allowed Said to observe the captives and think about what he would do with each one of them. He had some ideas, which he would share with Khaled later.

Callum, Jack and Patrick walked in silence, securely tied to the man or woman in front and behind. Twelve heavily armed guards made it futile to attempt escape, and if they did get loose where would they go? What each of the three young men did do was look with keen eyes at everything around them, memorising as much as they could of the surroundings, the buildings and streets.

Finally, they arrived at a large building and stopped at a door. The captives looked up to see a building with two floors and few windows. It was bigger than any building Callum and Jack had ever been inside, even bigger than their church. Patrick thought the same, although perhaps it was about the size of Baltimore Castle, the useless structure that kept those inside safe, those men who did nothing to help the people of the town on the day they were taken a week ago. This building stretched along the street for over 100 paces either side of the great door, then seemed to form corners and continue back beyond what they could see from where they stood. The few windows gave it a sombre look and Patrick wondered how dark it must be inside.

Khaled walked up to the door and with his small club banged on it three times.

"Mehmed, Mehmed, open the door. We have returned with our prize."

They could hear the bolts being moved, keys being turned and the door was opened from inside. A man stood in the doorway. He was large in every sense, tall and round, no longer in his youth but not yet old. A smile appeared on his face, revealing a mouth with only half of its teeth still present and his body odour suggested he clearly didn't care to wash every day.

"Welcome back Khaled, I see you've been busy, bring my new guests in."

Mehmed laughed at his own joke and stepped aside to allow Khaled to lead them all through the doorway. As Khaled walked past Mehmed he pulled a face.

"Mehmed, you smell like the pigs the infidel eat, when did you last wash your body?"

"Washing isn't important for my work Khaled; the Pasha doesn't visit me and the whores don't complain." He was still smiling but spat the words out as the captive women walked past.

Once through the doorway the sixty-five captives and oarsmen were lined up in a courtyard, where they were made to stand and wait in the middle, which was not shaded from the sun. Said and Khaled had gone to one side and sat down at a table, where they ate some food, brought to them by a young woman of European appearance. The ten Corsair guards moved to the side into the shade, where they also received refreshment.

"Come Anna, have you missed me?"

Khaled beckoned to the serving girl and as she moved forward he grabbed her arm and pulled her close. The captives stood and watched as he spoke to her and they could see her attempt at a smile for Khaled was false and that she was scared.

"I will see you later Anna, although we might have found a replacement for you."

Khaled smiled as he spoke and glanced over at Laura and Mary.

"But the problem with that is we won't need you here anymore, so we'll take you down to the market."

The girl tried to show no emotion but her discomfort was plain. Laura and Mary couldn't understand what was said by Khaled but the glance he gave them and the look on the girl's face gave them some idea. Khaled was enjoying himself.

"Hey Mehmed, perhaps you could afford Anna and have her for yourself."

Khaled laughed and the big overseer looked up at Khaled and leered at the girl, increasing her discomfort.

"That's enough Khaled. Stop scaring her, you can enjoy yourself later."

Once again Said had to intervene and he wanted to get on with business. This consisted of deciding who they would keep and who they would sell. Said liked to have the strongest young men and if he was keeping women he chose the ones he liked.

"We will keep up to forty oarsmen and possibly five girls, the rest can go to market."

Khaled nodded, he agreed with Said on virtually everything, the exception being discipline, on which he thought his friend and brother was too soft. Khaled could do simple arithmetic and the sale of twenty slaves would make them both wealthy. They were becoming known as one of Algiers' most effective team of slavers, and if they carried out three or four big raids like these last two every year, they would be soon be known by the Sultan himself.

After discussing which of the men and women they would keep, they got Mehmed and a few of the Corsairs to separate the slaves into two groups, which saw the sixteen men and four women who would not be kept by them being led to two rooms close to the great door; men in one, women in the other. All the time Callum, Jack, Laura, Mary and the others watched, then they were led to the other end of the courtyard, through a door into a large room that contained what was best described as three cages. The forty men were divided into two groups and placed in the two larger cages, where once inside and the cage door was secured and they were released from their shackles by holding their arms forward through the bars of the cage. Then the five women were placed in the smallest cage and also released from their shackles. The door of the room was closed, they could hear it being locked and then it was silent. For the first time since they were all seized, either at sea, in Mevagissey, or in Baltimore, they were not under the gaze of Corsairs or in fear of the overseer's whip.

Deep breaths could be heard from each cage and finally Jack broke the silence.

"Where are we, does anyone know?"

"Be careful English boy, keep your voice low, or he'll be in here with whip and club."

The voice had an accent but he spoke good English.

"Sorry Sir, who is he, and who are you?"

Jack said these words quietly and the conversation continued at a hushed level.

"I am Pedro. I'm Portuguese and have been here for maybe three months. The big man with the whip is Mehmed and he's the Basha. Be careful of him, he is big and stupid but also cruel and brutal. The two men who led the raids that brought you here are Said and Khaled. They own this Bagno but Said is the brains and makes the decisions. Be careful of Khaled though, he can be as bad as Mehmed."

"We know."

Jack replied and glanced through the bars of the cage, towards Laura in the small cage. Then continued the conversation.

"What is a Basha and what is a Bagno Pedro?"

"A Bagno is the name for a slave prison in cities all along the Barbary Coast. They can be huge, like the one here in Algiers that belongs to the Grand Pasha, who serves the Sultan in Istanbul. This one is small, owned by Said and Khaled, which is good for us as it's not so crowded, so we are less likely to die of disease. Said is a better slave owner than most, he doesn't want you to die, he wants you to live and work for him. A Basha is the slave overseer in charge of the slaves kept in each Bagno. Unfortunately for us we've got Mehmed. If Said is not around and Mehmed has been drinking alcohol or smoking hashish, then you will see the darker side of him. When he's like that the women should be very careful to stay in the shadows."

Pedro said the last sentence quietly but Laura and the others heard. She looked around in the fading light to see she shared the small cage, with just Mary and three other young women. All the other women who had been taken captive from Megavissey and Baltimore had been separated and placed in a room at the other end of the courtyard.

"Why have we been separated from the others?"

Laura asked quietly not wanting to draw the attention of the man they now knew as Mehmed. Pedro couldn't quite hear her but one of the other women could and spoke in her Italian-English.

"They will be sold and we will be kept Signora."

"Thank you, Miss. My name is Laura and this is Mary."

Lucia moved closer so the five women could speak with some privacy, without the men in the two cages hearing them. Eventually they all settled down as best they could to get some sleep. Before he fell asleep Callum, who had been watching the five women whispering, could hear one of them crying and could hear muffled words of comfort spoken by the other four.

Pedro had explained to the new men what was happening, as Lucia did to Laura and Mary. They were all awake at sunlight and none had slept well, largely because although their hands had been released from shackles, their ankles had remained chained all night. Clearly no chances would be taken and it would be impossible to run as one of twenty men chained together. It wouldn't even work for the five women.

As Pedro had predicted Mehmed appeared with two women carrying a large bowl full of a soup or broth, as well as some smaller bowls. They were passed through the bars of the cage allowing four to five men to eat, then the small bowls were refilled and passed to the others. Bread was brought through from the courtyard and finally water. As there were forty men and five women the process took longer than Mehmed had expected, he became agitated and turned on one of the women.

"Hurry up old woman, I haven't got all day to stand here while you feed the infidel dogs."

With that he waved his club and knocked the unfortunate woman off her feet, taking care not to hit her about the head. She lay on the floor for a short time, before gathering herself and getting to her feet to resume her duty, as if nothing had happened. Laura looked at the poor woman and wondered where she had been taken from and how long she'd be held in this building called a bagno.

The identity of the old woman was known by a few but it was unimportant, no-one cared. She was largely anonymous and served a simple but important function, preparing and serving food to the occupants of the bagno. Said knew that her name was Madeline and she was taken from a French ship sailing to Italy twenty-eight years earlier in 1603. She was part of the package when he and Khaled bought the bagno from Abdul, and she was an essential component in the smooth running of the operation. To almost everyone else she was simply known as the old woman and other worse names. Only the recent arrival of the slave girl Anna saw any change to this, and for the first time in years there was someone who spoke kindly to her.

Madeline had lived in the bagno since being taken captive and brought to Algiers by Abdul, and had never been outside the building since that day. The effect of this incarceration and her treatment led to an erosion of dignity and self-respect. When she was taken she was nearly thirty years of age, the mother of three children, who were the joy of her life. Madeline had initially missed her children and her husband desperately and lived in the hope she might one day be reunited with them. The French mother was an attractive woman and was brought back to the bagno for Abdul's pleasure, which she did for seven years, after which her looks began to fade and Abdul lost interest, replacing her with a younger woman. Then she had to perform the same role for various Corsairs who lived in the bagno.

Finally, after twelve years as a concubine Madeline was no longer desirable to any of the men and she was given the job of preparing food when the previous old woman died. Once she was of no use as a concubine, Madeline was often the subject of cruel jokes and humiliation from the men she came into contact with, particularly if they had been drinking. The only exception was Said, who could see she was important and he would sometimes thank her for bringing him food. Madeline learnt to avoid eye contact or any conversation with the men, fulfilling her tasks when commanded.

But by the time twenty years had passed she had given up hope of ever seeing her children again. Any pride she had disappeared and she lived from one day to the next working for the masters, knowing there was always the chance of the occasional assault like that meted out by Mehmed. Her treatment as a concubine until she was no longer desirable, followed by years of insults and assaults as a domestic servant, led to her becoming old before her time. She was a working part of the bagno that no-one cared about and she moved about the building with the freedom of a ghost. Many of the men didn't even notice her presence if she was nearby and would talk openly about things they might have been more guarded about around other people. Madeline could have been a piece of furniture.

Madeline was resigned to never leaving the bagno and spent most of every day in the kitchen. Her sleeping area was a small ante-room attached to the kitchen and she came to feel secure and safe, albeit a prisoner. In 1631 and in her fifty-fifth year, her memories of her children were disappearing and she had learnt that emotions were a luxury inside the bagno that led to misery. Madeline's strategy for surviving became a daily routine of preparing and serving food, not looking directly at anyone, particularly the masters and Mehmed, staying anonymous and silent.

Five days later Laura, along with everyone in the bagno, witnessed further humiliation of Madeline, again at the hands of Khaled. Dinner had been served, the male captives were being exercised by Mehmed and a few Corsairs, as Khaled and Said sat under a shelter eating, drinking and observing.

"Old woman, come here and clean up this mess."

Khaled was referring to the mess he'd left at the table he shared with Said, which Madeline started to wipe up, but unfortunately she spilt something over Khaled's leg.

"Stupid bitch! Are you incapable of following instructions?"

He bellowed at her from just an arm's length, so loud that everyone in the bagno could hear, drawing everyone's attention. Khaled towered over her and continued to scream

"Is it time you were replaced, old woman? How could Abdul ever have found you desirable, or fit for his bed."

With that he raised his hand to strike her but was stopped by Said.

"Leave her Khaled, she made a mistake. Besides we need her, otherwise we could all starve."

Said hoped some humour in his voice might save the old woman.

"Be careful or she might poison your food one day."

Khaled wasn't ready to see the humour.

"Listen old bitch, if you poison me I promise you, Mehmed and the guards will flay you alive. Do you understand me hag?" Again, he was standing over Madeline, screaming at her.

No blows were landed or needed, Madeline cowered, turned away, lowering her head, like a submissive dog that had been beaten so many times it had no resistance. Everything was witnessed by the captives in silence. The watching Corsairs showed little interest, although a few of them found it amusing. Anna was stood in the shadows, avoiding Khaled's eye in case he should turn on her. Madeline stood still as they all watched, she was waiting for Khaled to finish her humiliation, 'It will be alright, it will be over soon, then I can go to the kitchen', she thought to herself. Finally, Said could not bear it anymore.

"That's enough Khaled, Madeline go to the kitchen and clear-up."

This was the life of the old woman Laura saw beaten by the overseer.

Lucia

Lucia, a young Italian woman of twenty-four years, was captured when her father's merchant ship was seized sailing from Venice to Marseilles.

The favourite child of Fabrizio Broggi, a wealthy trader and member of Venice's Grand Council, Lucia had become his trusted notary and was travelling to France to speak on his behalf to merchants who might import his products. Fabrizio's trust in his daughter was complete, she had a sharp sense for business and could speak five languages, their own Italian, French, Spanish, German and even English. These skills in languages made her invaluable in commercial deals he hoped to make across Europe, whether it be selling silk from the East, fine Italian wine, English wool, or anything else that might make a profit.

Lucia's education had started at the age of nine studying languages, showing a natural flair. By the time she was fourteen she was shadowing her father in the trade halls and coffee shops of Venice. Fabrizio was happy to have his beloved daughter at his side, his wife having died when Lucia was seven. He could ensure she was safe and by the time she was seventeen she was advising him about the business. Her counsel was valued and other families respected their relationship, with Lucia somehow rising above being a beautiful daughter to be married-off.

Every important family in Venice knew the Broggi family and every son in those families admired Lucia. There was even talk of her being married into the family of the Doge. By 1631 Lucia was twenty-four years of age and some thought she was getting old, Fabrizzio didn't care. Lucia didn't need a match, she was different to the other young wealthy women, strong in character and independent. Fabrizzio would have liked grand-children and Lucia herself admired many handsome men, but she didn't feel desperate for a husband and she enjoyed working in the family business. Fabrizzio wondered if she might be best suited to a man ten years older than her who wouldn't feel threatened by her independence, perhaps a widower.

'We can talk about it when she gets back from Marseille', he thought to himself, 'but then I've been thinking that for several years now.'

As Fabrizzio watched his ship leave Venice he thought they should all sit down and talk about the future, not just Lucia's but also Francesco's and that of the business, which he had tried to do several times before. Fabrizzio had grown tired of sea voyages but sent his son, Francesco, to accompany and protect Lucia. She was clever and carried his seal, conveying authority on his behalf, but she was still a woman in a man's world. Francesco was strong and loyal, loved his sister and would defend her with his life, but he knew she was the one with the brains and an understanding of commerce. They made a good team to take the family business forward and Fabrizzio had faith in them.

Two days out of Venice the world of the Broggi family crashed when two ships appeared from the south. They could see them from a long way off, everyone became nervous as the two ships closed in on them quickly, before there was any time to turn back towards Italy. No one needed to speak, they all knew they were Corsairs as soon as the oars of the two galleys became visible.

Lucia and Francesco became two more slaves amongst thousands taken and held in Algiers in 1631. Their lot wasn't as severe as it was for many for two reasons. First, if they weren't killed then surely their father would find out and would pay a ransom. Trinitarian and Mercedarian priests were present in Algiers, religious orders from Italy whose sole purpose was to negotiate the freedom of Italian captives. Secondly, although they didn't know it, they were captives of Said, who had plans for them both and wasn't intending to sell them in the Algiers slave market. Lucia and Francesco had been captured by Said and Khaled on their previous voyage, the one before setting off for England and Ireland. By the time of the Corsair's return the two young Italians had been held captive in Algiers for two months.

For the first few days nothing much seemed to happen, allowing everyone held in the cages to get to know each other. They were taken out to the courtyard to walk and breathe fresher air than they had inside the locked rooms with poor ventilation. Food and water were provided twice a day, which was sufficient as they were not doing any work.

These few days allowed Said, Khaled and their ten Corsair guards to rest and recover from the voyage. Despite all of them being experienced at being at sea, these long raids were always tiring and sleeping on dry land in a secure building was always preferable to sleeping at sea in a small space with twenty other men and even more slaves. These Corsairs liked serving under Said; he treated them well, developing a strong sense of loyalty. He was intelligent and would avoid potentially dangerous situations if at all possible, qualities that meant his men were more likely to all return home. Despite the bravery and showmanship of Khaled the Corsairs had a greater respect for the quieter, more measured decision-making of Said. "Less rape and pillage, but less likely to die," older experienced Corsairs would point-out to their younger colleagues.

A few days of rest also allowed Said to talk to Khaled about his plans for their captives, which he'd mentioned before but could now explain in more detail.

"Listen Khaled, we should build up a bagno which will become known throughout the empire as having the best slaves. We don't need to fill our galleys with old or weaker men, who may or may not sell quickly. Similarly, with the women, we should seize only the most beautiful, like those five we now have across the courtyard."

Said looked at Khaled to see his response to this last detail, as he knew Khaled enjoyed taking women captives, particularly if they weren't being sold to a Pasha and other wealthy buyers who demanded maidens.

"This means we take young beautiful girls and women, who are pure and untouched. Khaled you know that fair-skinned maidens fetch the highest prices. We want the Sultan himself to be speaking of our bagno and of the quality of our women."

"Said, I understand your reasoning and you are far more clever than me, but please my brother, let me have one or two."

Khaled spoke with a smile, trying to make light of his needs, but inside he was irritated. Said would make their enterprise all business and no pleasure. Also, Khaled could not get the girl they had taken captive on her wedding day out of his head. He had been looking at her since the raid and promised himself he would have her for his pleasure, one way or another.

"Khaled, we can get you a couple of girls, you can have your own little harem if you wish. Please brother, leave those five alone, their price will fall if they are not maids."

"Enough, enough Said, I understand. Am I never to enjoy the spoils of our trade?"

Khaled's smile disappeared and he looked resigned. Said tried to cheer him up.

"Besides, you've got Anna, she's a beautiful girl who can satisfy all your needs."

The two best friends moved the conversation on from the women and agreed on arrangements for the men. Said's plan was that they would keep raiding but always keep the best captives for themselves, sending any others straight to the market. As their stock of big, strong, young men grew, they would sell the excess they didn't need in the market for the highest prices. Said explained to Khaled that if they sold only the best at high prices, they didn't need to sell as many as they would if they were selling more slaves at lower prices.

Khaled nodded and smiled again, his mood lifting. He forgot about the women and began to think about the gold and silver.

"Said, my brother, you are a great Corsair and as skilled a merchant as any Jew."

The result of this plan for their bagno meant that they would hold captives for longer before selling them. This meant they needed to devise a routine for the men and women. Leaving them to rot in the cages for weeks or months would result in their stock deteriorating and falling in value. Khaled was able to make a contribution here, which Said appreciated. "I have an idea you might like Said."

All of the captives would be exercised daily, walking and running in the courtyard. Khaled had connections through his family with the craftsmen who were building a new corner to the Pasha's fortress in the south-west corner of the city. He was able to arrange for the men to do some hard labour on a daily basis. Permanent hard labour for slaves eventually resulted in exhaustion and an early grave, unless they had a specialised skill, but two or three days a week would help to keep them strong. Also, the Pasha's notary would pay Khaled some gold or silver for the work carried out by a small team of ten to fifteen men each day. This small income would pay for food and drink to sustain the slaves. Said smiled and put his arm around his bigger friend's broad shoulders. "This is good Khaled." He was delighted with the idea and convinced his friend that spending just a little more on food would help to keep the sale price of their slaves high.

The women would exercise to keep their beauty and be kept out of the sun in the middle of the day. Anna and the old woman would bathe them and apply oils for their skin. It was well-known that European women who were exposed to too much sun seemed to lose their beauty quickly, their skin eventually turning brown and wrinkled like leather.

This regimen was set in place straightaway and Mehmed was initially confused at his masters' apparent softness. He had worked with slaves for years, being firm and severe if needed was always the best approach. However, his opinion didn't matter and he liked his masters, as they had never beaten him like previous ones. Perhaps Said's new ideas would work, but he was going to keep a close eye on these strong young men, as well as an even keener eye on the young women.

No information was fed through to the captives but they quickly became aware of a change. Some of those who had been in the bagno for a while, like Pedro, were the first to realise things were different. Whereas recent arrivals like Callum, Jack, Laura and Mary, weren't to know life in the bagno was any different to normal.

Khaled organised the men for two days of hard labour each week working on the fortress. They were sent in groups of twelve to fifteen, tied and shackled, as well as being escorted by eight Corsairs. It was hard work but after two weeks the men realised it was a routine they could cope with, particularly when they compared themselves to other men they laboured alongside. Several were seen to collapse from exhaustion and would be dragged away by guards. Few, if any, were seen to return.

The new captives came to learn how their bagno's slave operation worked. After some weeks thirty-two of the men were taken off to the harbour and found themselves back in the galleys. They were gone for only six days and all returned with one or two young Italians. A successful raid of a Venetian merchant ship provided a prize of wines and silks, as well as seven captives out of a crew of twelve. Five who had resisted, or were considered useless, were despatched into the Mediterranean, and five went straight to the market on the galley's return to Algiers. This went on for two months, during which there were three shipping raids, for which Said rotated the crews, taking care to observe the men and their performance as oarsmen.

All of the captives, male and female, were able to learn words in Arabic, making it easier to understand their masters, as well as a kind of slave-master lingua franca language. This consisted of words from Arabic, Italian and Spanish, which the English and Irish captives struggled with compared to the captives from Mediterranean countries, but they all learnt it to some degree, particularly the simple commands used by the masters and the basha.

Laura, Lucia and Mary, along with the other two young women, a Polish girl called Edyta, and a Spanish girl called Paola, became close and supported each other as much as they could in the circumstances. Edyta and Paola, who were finding the loss of their liberty and uncertainty of their futures very harrowing, struggled the most. Their emotions and tears were more evident than the other three. Lucia and Paola were particularly good at teaching the other three the Arabic-Latin lingua franca but it was clear Paola was struggling to cope with captivity more than the others.

Laura thought about Megavissey, her parents and Will every day, but found the company of the other women a focus for her mind. She decided she would survive, she owed it to Mary, John and Will. The sight of Khaled was a constant reminder of their deaths, somehow, she had to survive. He was also a source of hatred burning inside, but instead of letting it destroy her, she was determined to live to somehow avenge their deaths.

Paola was to be found weeping in the corner of the cage furthest from the men's cages and Laura would sit with her, holding her hand. The young Spanish woman was without hope, she faced a future a concubine, her honour would be taken against her will and she would never see her family again. As their ability to converse improved, Laura realised what she feared, which was that Paola did not want to live.

"I will kill myself, rather than be sold as a slave and have my honour taken by a pig like Khaled."

Paola whispered these words to Laura through tears and a face that had no hope or fight.

"No Paola, please. We must all fight and survive. Your family will not have given up hope of freeing you. Your country pays ransoms to free its people."

"I admire your hope Laura but ransoms take time and we could be sold next week."

"Don't give up Paola."

Paola looked at her new friend and wondered how she could be so strong. The events of Megavissey had been whispered and shared amongst the captives before Laura had chosen to tell the other women. What struck them all was the way Laura had been able to talk about it, a series of factual statements, without emotion. It was as if a piece of her life had come and gone, a chapter was over but she would carry on.

Since that day in Megavissey Laura had not cried, nor had she laughed, her emotions had been paralysed. However, Laura found herself guided by emotion again. She cared about the other women, she cared about staying alive, she cared about revenge. She decided she was not weak, she was strong and determined. It was these feelings that made her Paola's crutch, who she helped and consoled whenever the Spanish girl needed her. With Mary it was different. She and Laura were like equals, twin sisters, both mentally and physically strong. Mary was aware of Laura's care for Paola and admired her, particularly in view of the events during her capture in Cornwall. If Laura wanted to tell her more about her life in Megavissey before the raid Mary would listen, but it didn't happen, Laura chose not to.

After weeks of Paola talking of suicide, Laura began to achieve progress in persuading her there was always hope. Paola began to be less tearful and a smile would sometimes appear on her pretty face, giving Laura great satisfaction, but she still couldn't smile or laugh herself. She decided it didn't matter, she was focused on survival and revenge.

Each evening after they had been fed and they were confined to their cages, the men would talk and look at the women. Their stares weren't lustful like those of Khaled and Mehmed, more modest and sympathetic. The men had never seen five more beautiful women but their thoughts were not carnal, they feared for these young women, thinking about where they might end up and under whose control they might live. Callum could not take his eyes off Laura and found himself thinking of her most of the day, particularly when out labouring at the Pasha's fortress. The image of her in his mind helped him get through the day and at night he thought of her as he fell asleep. He realised he adored her but knew he was destined to never know her.

Anna

The women captives got more of an idea of what was to happen to them from two unlikely sources. The slave girl Anna, who attended to the five women each day, was happy to build a relationship, which became a friendship. She had been seized at sea six months earlier and had become Khaled's concubine. The sadness in her eyes made them all feel for Anna but she assured them it wasn't as bad as it could be. Khaled had taken her honour and he could be unkind but he wasn't violent, providing she did what he wanted willingly. Importantly, Anna had been present several times when Said and Khaled had discussed their plans.

"They have special plans for the five of you. They want you to look as beautiful as possible, as they intend to sell you to rich, powerful men in the Ottoman Empire."

Paola burst into tears at the thought of what lay ahead.

"Paola, this isn't so bad. You are beautiful and will be one of many in a wealthy man's harem. If you become his favourite and you give him children, you will be treated like a queen and live in luxury for the rest of your days. If you're not his favourite, you will have a quiet life as one of many in the harem, known by only one man who might require you to pleasure him once a month. Listen to me, do it well, please him and your future will be secure."

The five young women listened intently.

"What about the men over there."

Mary asked the question and glanced over towards her brother Patrick.

"Said wants to have the best captives along the Barbary Coast. Like you, he is keeping them because he thinks they will fetch a high price, or he will keep them himself for his own galleys."

Mary's head dropped at the thought that she might be separated from her brother and he could end up on an Ottoman galley.

"When will all this happen. When will we and they be sold?"

Anna could see the fear of the future in Mary's face and tried to reassure her.

"I don't know for certain Mary but I will listen to their conversations as much as possible."

This and further conversations with Anna helped Mary to clear her mind of any uncertainty regarding their futures. It was just a matter of when.

Then during the second of the raiding voyages that took Said and Khaled away from the bagno for another five days, the five women and the remaining men learnt some more from, of all people, Mehmed.

The big overseer had been clearly briefed by Said regarding the captives, particularly the women. Said and Khaled knew he had a problem controlling his emotions, both in terms of brutality towards the men and molestation of the women. He had a history and in the past Said had threatened to flay him alive for the rape of a girl from Greece. She immediately lost half her value in the market and was sold at a much lower price to the owner of a brothel. Mehmed had been thrown into a punishment pit reserved for difficult captives and left to think about the cost for three days.

Unfortunately, Mehmed had a weakness for both hashish and alcohol. One evening the five women were in the bathing room with Anna and the old woman. Having been washed they were having oils applied to keep their skin soft. Mehmed had watched the whole process through a small gap where the door was held on its hinges. He knew from the incident with the Greek maid that he was forbidden from touching them but he could not control his emotions, not helped by the hashish and wine. Unable to stop himself, he burst into the room, causing alarm and panic as the women grabbed cloths to cover themselves. They stood still, frozen, looking down at the floor to convey modesty, as the overseer walked in carrying his whip in one hand. Anna spoke, trying to take control of the situation.

"Are you insane Mehmed, they will kill you for this."

With that Anna walked forward, placing herself between Mehmed and the five maidens. Any ability to apply reason and think through the consequences of his actions was sabotaged by alcohol and hashish. But his response was swift, punching the serving girl in the face. Anna fell to the floor, groaning with pain. She was useless to stop him and he walked up to the five captive women, barely able to control himself.

Mehmed knew he couldn't do what he wanted, which would definitely result in his execution, he was aware of Said's special plans for these girls. However, that did not mean he could not look and perhaps touch the flesh of a beautiful white woman bound for a rich man's harem.

"Look at you five, I'm a lucky man to see you in the flesh, thank you."

He laughed but none of the women spoke. They didn't know he wouldn't take one of them for fear of death.

Mehmed stroked the body of Laura with the handle of his whip, adding more fear to the five women. Lucia started to tremble and cry, which drew his attention to her. He placed his hand behind her neck and held her so close Lucia could smell his sweat and felt his foul breath.

"By Allah, perhaps death is worthwhile for the pleasure of having one of you."

Mehmed was losing control but was interrupted by the pained voice of Anna, who had gathered herself still laying on the floor. Blood was seeping from her lip.

"Mehmed, stop now, or you will pay for this with your life. I will tell Khaled."

Mehmed's passion turned to anger, he left Lucia where she stood crying, walked over to Anna, kicking her in the stomach, causing a scream of pain as she doubled up. The other women ran over to the poor slave to help her, which seemed to stop Mehmed and he stepped back, regaining some control.

"Say a word of this to Said or Khaled and I will tell them I caught you plotting the escape of the captives."

With that the overseer turned and left the bathing room, cursing under his breath.

Anna was helped by the other five and the wound to her mouth was gently cleaned with kindness. They were taken back to their cage by Anna, Mehmed reappeared to lock them in for the night, Anna went to her room and Corsair guards made sure the bagno was secure for the night. Everything was witnessed by someone who remained silent. The old woman only emerged from the shadows after everyone had left and cleared up the cloths on the floor.

This incident, whilst terrifying, led to Mary being focused on one thing. She knew they had to have a plan, which could somehow get them out of the bagno and out of Algiers. The women had much free time in their daily routine, allowing Mary to think and try to find a way for them to escape.

Five days after the incident with Mehmed in the bathing room, Said, Khaled and the thrity-two oarsmen returned to Algiers. Fortunately for Mehmed the cut to Anna's lip had largely healed and she chose to not say anything to Khaled. Evidently the voyage was not as successful as others, leaving Khaled in a bad mood. No captives were brought back to the bagno, as they were not of the quality required by Said, a small number taken instead straight to the market. This wasn't a bad thing as it meant Said and Khaled received more gold and silver to pay their Corsairs and buy food.

More of the men were learning the lingua franca and Arabic, resulting in more of them being able to pick up information from overheard conversations. By the start of their third month in the bagno the men and women knew it was a matter of time before all of the women and some of the men were sold.

Said became excited one morning as he received news of a visitor.

"Khaled, Khaled! He's coming to Algiers and has heard of us."

Khaled emerged from his room on the first floor and stood looking over the veranda.

"What and who are you talking about Said?"

He wiped the sleep from his eyes and without turning his head called.

"Anna, bring me some water."

Moments later Anna, wearing a night gown, came from his room with water looking embarrassed. It was clear to everyone in the courtyard what her role had been that night.

"Good girl Anna, now you can go to work. Feed the women captives."

Anna slipped away to begin her daytime duties.

"The Grand Pasha of Istanbul is coming to Algiers, Khaled. He wants to see our women."

Said was beaming, no-one had seen him happier. The fruits of his plan for their bagno were beginning to ripen. The two of them sat down at a table in the shade to discuss further what they would do to prepare for the visit of possibly the second most important man in the Ottoman Empire. None of the captives could hear the details of the conversation, as they sat eating and drinking, but everyone had heard the news as it was shouted between the courtyard and the veranda. However, there was one person who could hear some of what they discussed, the old woman who served them at their table.

After the assault by Mehmed and the kindness shown by the women, Anna's attitude began to warm towards the captives and she would whisper to them more information about how the bagno worked. She knew how many Corsair guards were on duty, where they were stationed and where they slept. Furthermore, the old woman, Madeline, would speak to her daily. They were the only two women who lived and worked in the bagno, preparing food and now looking after these 'special' women captives. Both of them despised Khaled and Mehmed. Madeline shared with Anna what she overheard when serving Said and Khaled, which Anna passed on to Laura and Mary.

"They are going on one more raid, in the hope of bringing back a few more men, maybe one or two women. They are going as part of a bigger group and are taking just one of their smaller, faster galleys. When they return they are going to prepare the bagno for the visit of the Sultan's Grand Pasha, who will be in Algiers looking for the best slaves to take back to Istanbul. Said hopes that will include at least one of you, maybe even all of you."

Anna said the last part with a sympathetic voice. She and they now understood that would be the end of any hope of freedom.

"What about the men?"

Mary asked, thinking of Patrick.

"Many of them will be sold. Said and Khaled will be rich with gold and silver. They will keep perhaps half of the men. Enough to power at least one galley, then start over again, looking for new young men and girls like you."

Anna had to leave and the five women were left to their thoughts and whispered conversation. Back in the cages, Mary looked across at Patrick and the other men. He could see the worried look on her face and was concerned but Mary couldn't tell him what was happening yet, not until she had a plan of escape. That was the beginning, the modest start of Mary's plot to get them out of this place, before they were sold and sent to distant corners of the Ottoman Empire. 'Dear God, Jesus and Mary, what can we do', she thought to herself, her mood being less than confident but she was determined to come up with something. Over the course of the next few days the young Irishwoman was quieter than normal, it was noticeable how pensive she had become. 'The masters will be away, Mehmed will be in charge. He's big and repulsive but he's got his weaknesses', she told herself. 'Mehmed is the key to us getting out and yes, he's got the keys to the cages'. 'Mehmed's weaknesses….'

If they spoke quietly at night, they could communicate between the cages and Mary was able to let Patrick and the other men know what they'd learnt from Anna. Everyone in the two men's cages listened intently in silence. Mary had an idea but it required a great risk and chance. However, she was not going to share it with the men until Said and Khaled had gone on the next raid. She could not risk one of those taken to row deciding to try and use the revelation of her plan as a bargaining tool to secure his release. It also meant she might never see Patrick again if he was part of the small crew and the rest of them were successful in their escape. She shared her plan and discussed it with the other four women. Then all she could do was pray every night that Patrick was not chosen to go on the raid.

Two weeks passed, then all of the men were called into the courtyard. Said and Khaled came out fully armed, joined by ten Corsairs, also armed for carrying out a raid.

"So sixteen of you are coming on a raid with us for a few days."

Khaled called out so everyone in the bagno could hear, including the women, who could see the selection process through the small window to their room. Mary's heart raced, she closed her eyes and prayed that Patrick wouldn't be chosen. Laura could see her anguish and held Mary's left hand in both of hers. She knew what her friend feared and willed that Patrick would not be chosen.

Khaled went down the line tapping the shoulder of the men he wanted to take. As he approached Callum, Jack and Patrick he raised his whip to indicate all three, completing the twelve they required. Mary watching let out a groan and almost collapsed in Laura's arms but the selection by Khaled was interrupted by Said.

"Khaled, we've seen what those three can do on several voyages now. I know they will fetch a good price in the market, or we might even keep them here. Let's see what some of the others can do at sea."

With that Khaled nodded his head, Said was right and he liked the idea of testing some of the others. He lowered his whip and walked over to three of the youngest men who were seized in the raid on Baltimore. Pointing at them he gave his command.

"You three, over here."

Mary was able to catch her breath and her heart stopped pounding. Patrick was not going, which gave her hope for her plan. She also felt some sorrow for the three young men she knew from home. If she and Patrick made it back to Baltimore, she pictured in her mind having to tell the families of the three boys what their fate was. But for the moment Mary was left with a great sense of relief, Patrick was staying, the masters would be gone for at least five days, maybe more, leaving them that long to hatch her plan and escape.

Within ten minutes they were gone; Said, Khaled, ten Corsairs and sixteen oarsmen.

That night when they had all been locked in the cages, Mary was able to explain her plan and why they had to escape before the return of their masters. All of the remaining twenty-four men listened and nodded their agreement. None of them felt confident about life if they remained there in Algiers. They had been treated better than other slaves they saw doing hard labour but it was clear to them all that they could easily be sold to anyone, for any purpose. If the escape Mary had planned was successful in getting them out of the bagno, some of the men had a good knowledge of the streets which could lead them out of the town.

What they needed now was Mehmed to do what he always did when the masters were away.

Mehmed

Two days after the masters had left Mehmed was again relaxing in his familiar way, starting with some hashish, followed by wine. For once the women in the bagno were pleased to hear from Anna that that he was back to his old ways. They had a plan that would rely on him being under the influence of two of his vices, leading to him pursuing a third vice.

He was sitting in the courtyard enjoying some Italian wine Said had brought back from a raid and as usual, after some wine, his thoughts turned to the women captives and Anna. Then to focus his mind even more he could hear them in the bathing room, which was unusual as they were normally quiet, not wanting to draw the attention of him, Khaled or the Corsairs. Tonight was different, there was laughter, it sounded like the maidens were enjoying themselves, he became intrigued.

Mehmed didn't need further prompting, pulled himself out of the chair, furtively looked around to see if anyone was watching, then crept around the side of the courtyard to the bathing room door, which was ajar. He paused outside to listen, standing as close to the door as he could without revealing himself to those inside.

Having stood there for a few minutes the sounds were irresistible, he had to peer through the opening and Mehmed was met by a sight he'd only ever seen in one of his fantasies. The five captives were naked and attending each other with cloths and sponges in a way that was erotic and arousing. They were clearly enjoying the touches they gave each other, which resulted in girlish giggles and laughter. Anna seemed to be orchestrating the bathing and would join the other five, wiping their breasts with a soapy cloth, resulting in looks of rapture on the faces of the women. For Mehmed it was the most beautiful thing he had ever witnessed and he was transfixed, unable to move.

Unlike before, when he was noticed by the women, they smiled, laughed and only turned away after a few moments, allowing him to see and absorb in his mind the kind of scene he imagined only Sultans and Pashas enjoyed. He was hooked and couldn't help himself, quietly walking into the room, closing the door behind him.

Anna turned around and teased him.

"Do you like what you see Mehmed? Would you like to join us?"

The women giggled, smiled and turned away, a gesture to modesty.

He walked slowly towards the naked women, unable to speak but couldn't stop himself from holding out his hand, wanting to touch one of them.

"Be careful Mehmed, if you're seen or heard by the guards, you know Said and Khaled will be severe in their punishment."

"Let me just touch you, no more, I promise."

Anna couldn't believe she was talking with this pig of an overseer who had treated her and Madeline so cruelly in the past. But this was all according to Mary's plan.

Mehmed was desperate to touch Laura and stroked her hair, causing revulsion inside the young woman, but somehow, she manged to smile, suggesting to the big overseer both willingness and pleasure. He started to tremble and sweat not knowing what to do next.

"Why don't you come to us later Mehmed, in a while when we are back in our room. It will be quiet and the guards will be resting. I will be there with them."

Anna was offering Mehmed something he'd only dreamed of. Any rational reasoning in his head was gone, he couldn't resist and must go to them.

"Yes Anna, yes. You're right, there are too many ears here. I will come and visit you in a short while."

He wasn't looking at any one of them in particular, he was speaking to all of them, any one of them would be enough. Mehmed left the bathing room and went back to his table the other side of the courtyard, sat down alone with his wine and his thoughts. His head was spinning.

Darkness soon covered the bagno, the five women were locked in their cage and the curtain that separated them from the men's cages was drawn, providing some privacy. Anna sat and waited in the shadows and looked reassuringly at the others.

"What if he falls asleep from drinking too much wine?"

Lucia was nervous and her concern was shared by the others. If their chance was missed tonight it might be too late, as the masters could return anytime.

"Don't worry, we will have at least two more nights, the masters rarely come back from a raid after just three nights at sea. And didn't you see his face in the bathing room, I am certain he will be here very soon, as he will also be thinking this is his chance before they return."

Anna was more confident than the others, perhaps because she knew him better, whereas they just saw him as a cruel repulsive beast. So they had to sit and wait, which they did in silence, they all knew what to do.

It was getting late but none of them had fallen asleep as the tension in their heads and bodies was far too great. They could hear some of the men snoring across the room and Mary smiled to herself at the thought of her brother sleeping as the women were going to attempt to get them all free. Nothing new there she thought to herself, the women doing the work while the men sleep. The humour of the situation made her feel she was still human, made her think of home. Maybe there was hope, perhaps they could get back to Ireland, anywhere, just out of captivity. But in one matter she was wrong, Patrick was not asleep, nor was Callum. They knew from the whispers after lights were extinguished that tonight could be the night for Mary's plan, but it could be the next night, or the next. None of the men knew of the details of Mary's plan, just that they would need to be ready to go when told. Neither Callum or Patrick could sleep, they both feared what could happen to the women if the plan failed. Feeling helpless locked in their cage, both young men felt their stomachs tying in knots with nervous tension. Patrick would fight and die for his sister and Callum was feeling the same for Laura. But they could do nothing locked in their cage and had to trust these two strong, determined, young women to deliver an opportunity for them all to escape from captivity.

As soon as darkness fell the silence was broken by the rustling noise of feet shuffling across the courtyard. Then they were aware of the door opening slowly and Mehmed entering carrying a light. He was breathing heavily and walked over to the right-hand side of the room, adjacent to the women's cage and, thanks to the curtain, out of sight from the men.

He was unsure of what to do and seemed unsteady on his feet, suggesting he'd had more wine. Placing the lamp on the table, there was enough light for him to see the silhouettes of the women sitting in the cage, but the shadows prevented him from seeing the details of their faces and bodies.

"You told me to come to you."

His voice was uncertain. The big man was different in this situation, lacking the normal brash confidence of an overseer speaking to captives. He was more like an adolescent speaking to a group of girls for the first time, except these girls were caged.

Laura, Lucia and Mary all stood up and walked over to the bars of the cage. They were wearing thin night clothes and the shapes of their bodies were visible for Mehmed to see, causing him to gasp.

"So, you've come to see us Mehmed, we're pleased to see you."

Mary stood to the side of Lucia and ran her fingers through the beautiful Italian's hair. Lucia responded by taking hold of Mary's other hand, first kissing it and then placing it on her own breast. Lucia bent her head back and breathed heavily.

The response from Mehmed was astonishment, followed by a gasp, as he then pressed himself against the bars. He held the bars of the cage tightly, feeling irresistible urges of passion and desire.

"I can't enter your cage, I can't, it would result in my execution and you being sold as brothel whores."

"Don't worry Mehmed, none of us want to die, but we can still enjoy ourselves before the masters return."

With that Laura walked up behind Mary, placed both her arms around her and began to feel her breasts, drawing from Mary a look of rapture, of ultimate pleasure, all for Mehmed's benefit.

Both Lucia and Mary were causing Mehmed to lose his mind and he was pressing himself tight to the bars of the cage, reaching through with his arms, trying to touch the two women. As if answering his prayers they took two steps forward and he was able to place his hands on their bodies, touching their breasts, losing any self-control control he had left. It was for only seconds but seemed like an eternity for the two women, who had to hide the revulsion they felt in the pits of their stomachs.

Mehmed was transfixed feeling their breasts, then slowly moved his hands down their bodies, and in an instant, everything changed. With both of his arms out-stretched through the bars and both hands on Lucia and Mary, Mehmed realised Laura had come close as well but hadn't seen her reach through the bars to slip his dagger out of its scabbard attached to his belt. Mehmed's state of ecstasy blinded him to Laura's stealth and the next thing he felt was the dagger thrust into his stomach, applied by Laura with all her strength. Mehmed's reaction was to pull away from the cage but as Laura had buried the dagger into him, Lucia and Mary grabbed both arms, locking him against the bars. Mehmed let out a deep groan, before Anna came from behind stuffing an old rag into the overseer's mouth, preventing him from raising any alarm. He was frantically trying to pull himself away but Mary and Lucia held his arms with all their strength and Anna pushed him hard from behind against the bars. This allowed Laura to extract the dagger from his stomach, blood began to pour forth and she quickly moved up to his face, which was pressed firm against the bars of the cage. Looking into his eyes, Laura plunged the dagger deep into his neck and pulled it to the side, opening his throat. She let go and as his body slumped the weight of the huge overseer caused Mary and Lucia to lose their grip on his arms. It did not matter, Mehmed collapsed in a heap, stone dead.

For a moment the six women stood in silence and stared at the immense body. They looked at each other as if they did not know what to do next, just needing a moment to recover. The first part of Mary's plan had succeeded and across the room Callum and Patrick had been straining their necks to hear what was happening.

"What's happening Mary, are you alright?"

Patrick could not keep silent any longer and feared the worst hearing groans and the heavy thud of a body falling to the floor.

"Ssh Patrick, be quiet, we're taking care of it. Get everyone up and ready to go, but do it quietly, for God's sake."

Inside the cage the five women dressed quickly, while Anna took the keys from Mehmed's belt and opened the cages. The lamp Mehmed brought gave them light and the 24 men who emerged from the other two cages looked at the scene with astonishment. Patrick hugged his sister and Callum held Laura's hands in his.

"Sweet Jesus, you've done it Mary."

"Yes, and no thanks to you either," she retorted.

Their brother and sister banter had existed for 20 years and Mary saw no reason why it should end now.

"Are you alright Laura?"

This was all Callum could say and he looked at the blank haunted face of the young woman who had just killed a man. Laura was no longer weak and vulnerable but she still melted his heart.

Thus, was the first part of the plan successfully completed.

Escape

Having secured their release from the cages, Mary was happy to hand over leadership to Callum, who had listened to Pedro, the Portuguese, in the preceding days. Held captive in the bagno longer than any of the others, Pedro had more knowledge of the streets of Algiers.

He had gone to sea five months earlier and was older than many of the others. At home in a small town south of Lisbon he had tried various trades but struggled to support his family; his beautiful wife Vania and their darling daughter Camilla. The promise of making a great deal of money sailing the seas between Europe, Africa and the Americas seemed to be a solution to their problems and he joined a slavers ship sailing south towards Africa.

Pedro had thought about the morality of slaving and struggled for a while with his conscience, but in the end the necessity of providing for his family won the argument. 'Besides', he thought to himself, 'I'm not seizing these people and placing them in bondage. Nor am I selling them in the Americas. I'm just working on the ship to support my family'. Somehow the moral dilemma of making money from being involved in the African slave trade was excised from his reasoning, which he would later come to regret. At that earlier time he said goodbye to Vania and Camilla with a clear conscience one cool day in February 1631, sailing on the Santa Sofia bound for West Africa.

Pedro never realised the reality of taking African slaves on the perilous middle passage across the Atlantic. The Santa Sofia was seized by Said and Khaled when just two days south of the Sagres, the south-west tip of Portugal, sailing in open waters, not far from the coast of Morocco. There was a fight as the ship had an experienced and hardened crew, but they were no match for thirty Corsairs and most of the crew were killed, leaving Pedro and five other men to be taken back to Algiers. Pedro watched as the Santa Sofia was sunk, after it had been emptied of anything valuable or useful. Sitting in chains on the deck of the Barbary galley the horror of slavery and the irony of his situation struck him squarely between the eyes. Tears streamed down from the eyes of this big strong Portuguese, as he realised that he was to suffer the fate to which he had been prepared to subject others. He had heard many stories of Christian men being taken into slavery by Muslims, never to be seen again and his tears were also for the thought that he would never again see his beautiful Vania and Camilla. He wondered if this was God punishing him for thinking it was morally acceptable to profit from slavery. How could he ever have been so foolish? Were he able to go back four days he would never have stepped onto the Santa Sofia. But it was too late now for such regrets.

The voyage to Algiers gave him time to contemplate and think about what he should do. Firstly, he vowed to stay alive. Secondly, if he could escape he would seize the opportunity and thirdly, if anyone should ever speak favourably of slavery again, he would argue against the horror that was inflicted on men, whether they were black, white, Christian or Muslim. Pedro and two of his crewmates were taken to the bagno, the other three were never seen again, taken as he later realised straight to the slave market.

Anna and Madeline had been captives longer but it was testimony to their ordeal that they had never been outside the bagno since entering through the big wooden door. However, they did have a detailed knowledge of how the bagno was guarded, how many guards would be on duty and how many would be awake through the night. Madeline had joined them and for the first time in twenty-eight years grown men and women listened intently to what the old woman had to say.

By the time their whispered discussion had ended it was close to midnight. It was decided they would wait two more hours before trying to leave, by which time everyone, but two guards, should be asleep. One of the guards was by the big door, the other at the far corner. Madeline explained that both of them were likely to be half asleep but would stir at the slightest sound, the only people who might not cause them to raise an alarm would be Anna and herself. It was therefore agreed that the two serving women would walk up to the two guards, each with one of the men close behind. If asked why they were up at that time, they would say a couple of the women captives were unwell and they had been ordered to tend to any sickness, as Said did not want to lose the price they would fetch in the market at this late stage.

It was vital that the two guards be despatched as quietly as possible so Callum asked if anyone was skilled in cutting throats. No-one volunteered, they were seamen and farmers, not pirates or criminals.

"I will go with Madeline. Will someone go with Anna?"

No-one was keen to take on a trained Corsair single-handed, they had all seen what Barbary fighters could do. After a pause Oji, the tall African, stepped forward.

"Let me kill one of them."

After an hour or so the four of them slipped out of the large room and into the darkness of the courtyard. Madeline and Callum went to the right, towards the main door, Anna and Oji went to the left and the far corner of the courtyard. The remaining twenty-seven had to sit and wait, in complete silence, as if in prayer. Mary hugged Patrick and Laura held her head in her hands, praying they would escape and that Callum would return safely. She prayed for their return and their escape, but she also found herself praying for the brave young Englishman she had come to admire over the last three months.

Within three minutes the four of them returned, Callum and Oji both holding daggers with traces of blood. No sound had been heard and the bagno had remained silent.

"Those two will sleep well", said Oji.

They quietly made their way to the big door, stopping on the way at the weapons room. With Mehmed's keys they opened it with only the slightest of sounds. Each of them, women included, picked up an assortment of weapons. As they got to the door, Madeline gestured to stop and wait as she pointed to the kitchen, where she had spent much of the last 28 years. She slipped inside for only a minute, reappearing with six bags of food she had prepared over the last week.

Madeline leaned forward whispering to Mary and Anna.

"I can't go with you, I'm too old and will slow you down. I can stay and give them a false story about the direction you followed."

A tear appeared in her eye, showing that despite physical and mental abuse endured for more than a quarter of a century, she still had some emotions left. Mary stopped her, gently placing a finger over Madeline's lips.

"Madeline, you're coming with us. We all go, or none of us does. I'll ask one of the men to tie you up and take you out of this place in the same way you came in, so help me God."

Tears flowed from Madeline's eyes and Anna folded her arms around her whispering "Come, come with us Madeline." A faint smile appeared through her tears and Madeline joined them.

Four men gently lifted and unbolted the big main door, as if they were lifting a sleeping infant from its cot. Following Pedro, they filed out into the darkness and the streets of Algiers. The last two closed the door carefully knowing they might have four or five hours before their absence was noticed.

Walking in single file they hugged the walls in the darkness. It was a clear night and an almost full moon meant they could just see the buildings and streets they followed. Pedro led the way climbing uphill towards the south-west corner of the city. Fortunately, it was a route he and others had taken many times and would bring them to the place where they had been doing hard labour rebuilding the Pasha's fortress. Without the moonlight they would have been following their noses, in danger of getting lost. No-one spoke. They were well-armed but would prefer not to meet anyone, particularly Corsair guards. Thankfully having waited until the very darkest and quietest time of the night, some two hours before sunrise, their wish was realised and it seemed all of Algiers was asleep.

Before the visit of Mehmed, Pedro had discussed with the others earlier that evening what they would do if they got out of the city. It was agreed they would head south-west out of the city and uphill over the back of the cliffs that guarded the Bay of Algiers. The hillsides behind the clifftops were riddled with holes that led into the mass of rock. These were an infamous network of small passages that disappeared into the hillside, some led nowhere, but some would lead down to caves that opened out into the sea beside the Bay of Algiers. Pirates and smugglers had used these caves and passages for centuries and stories of boats being kept there were common around Algiers.

Not fancying their chances against a unit of trained Corsairs, the twenty-four men were confident they could cope with half a dozen or so, who might be guarding a boat. The hope was to seize a vessel of some kind and continue their escape across the sea. A boat with oars would be perfect as they had the skill and power to take on any galley that might pursue them.

At the unfinished fortress in the south-west corner of Algiers Pedro led them across and through the rocks that a few days before he and a hundred other slaves had worked on, hewing the stone into great blocks to build a wall. Surprisingly there were no guards present, perhaps they were laying down away from the rocks, where the ground was more kind for the purpose of sleeping. Once outside the city Pedro followed a stream, which flowed down the hillside, and after some time they were at the top of the hill, just as the sun began to rise.

Light appearing from the east made their progress easier but also filled them with a greater sense of nervousness, knowing that it wouldn't be long before the Corsairs raised the alarm back in the bagno. Fortunately, they knew the Corsairs never willingly got out of their beds earlier than necessary, preferring to wait until they were called by Khaled, Mehmed, or the old woman announcing that food was ready. Khaled was not there, hopefully still at sea and two or three days away. Mehmed and the two over-night guards would not be waking up, and Madeline was not there to wake the Corsairs with breakfast, so with luck they hopefully had a bit more time.

As they stopped to rest for a few minutes, to drink water and eat a little food, the mood was nervous but hopeful, they all knew this was their best chance of ever being free. Even Lucia and her brother, who had been hoping their father would pay a ransom for their freedom, were convinced that a ransom would arrive too late and Lucia would be bound for Istanbul, never to be seen again. After a short rest they pressed on and could look back at the city of Algiers in bright morning sunlight, all of them sharing the same thoughts of a beautiful sight but a place of so much misery and cruelty. They looked towards the west and hoped they would never see that city again.

Some four hours after leaving the bagno, walking across the hills at the back of the clifftops, they began to notice large holes in the hillside, through which somebody could crawl.

"These must be the gaps in the hillside which lead to the passages and caves," said Jack.

"Yes, the problem is into which one should we descend and will it lead us to a boat?" Pedro responded, pointing out the obvious but it needed saying.

From where they had stopped there were at least seven holes in sight and this seemed as good a place as any to try. Callum, Jack and Pedro talked about their next move, while the group rested.

"We can't all climb down into every hole, so let's choose five and send pairs of men down to see. We probably have at least the morning before they realise we have gone and guess we may have come up here. If we're lucky we might even have a couple of days."

Pedro's words relieved the nervousness they all shared. It was true, the Corsairs in the bagno might still be asleep and when they finally realised what had happened, it would not necessarily occur to them that the captives would come to the hillside looking for passages and caves. More likely they would have gone straight to the harbour, seized a ship and brazenly sailed out into the Bay of Algiers.

"Another thing to consider," Pedro continued, "is that the Corsairs in the bagno were left to guard and keep the masters' property secure, which they've failed to do. They will be very aware that if they don't find us and get us back in the cages before the return of Said and Khaled, there will be serious consequences for them. I don't think they will raise a city-wide alarm but they will try to find us themselves, quietly without raising an alarm."

Everyone in the group had gathered round to listen. Patrick spoke "You're right Pedro. Said and Khaled will not be best pleased when they start to work out how much gold and silver they've lost. What a pity Mehmed isn't alive to take the blame, his death would've been much slower."

Whilst still uncertain, the mood of the group had begun to lighten. Patrick in particular had been cheered up by the thought of Khaled setting about Mehmed, but he was cut short by Mary.

"We did enjoy his death Patrick. The look on his face was a joy to see."

Mary glanced over to Laura as she spoke seeing the satisfaction in the face of her friend. Unlike the others Laura was still unable to show that she could enjoy levity. Callum also noticed her cold resolve and wanted to put his arm around her, but this was neither the place or the time for him to reach out to her.

"Enough of Mehmed and the guards' fate. Let's get on. Who volunteers to crawl into the hillside?"

Callum was anxious to get everyone to safety, so the sooner they started the better. Within minutes five pairs of men chose holes and disappeared into the hillside. Those remaining sheltered under some olive trees on the side of the hill. Keeping an eye on Algiers, half expecting hordes of Corsairs to exit the city and charge up the hillside, the wait seemed an eternity. The sun was rising across the sky and it was early afternoon before the first pair emerged from their hole, followed shortly by two more pairs. All six men were scratched and bruised, looking disappointed at their failure to find a way down to the sea.

Two of the pairs reported dead-ends but the third hole, explored by two of the Irishmen Sean and Michael, did lead to a cave.

"We would be hidden and we could rest for a while. But there was no boat and if they came down looking for us we would be trapped." Sean was offering something but the look on his face showed little optimism.

The wait for the last two pairs seemed interminable but eventually the fourth pair appeared from the darkness in the hillside and they looked more hopeful.

"You've been gone a while, any luck?" Pedro was desperate for good news.

"Well we got to the sea and there's a cave for shelter. No boat but evidence of it probably being used by smugglers, or someone else."

Patrick threw down some tools he had found.

"The majority of us could wait down there while, say, eight of us went back into the city at night to steal a boat."

It was an idea but trying to get into Algiers unseen, steal a boat and then find the right cave in the cliffs, seemed a huge risk. Not to mention that by then their escape might be widely known by many and Corsairs would be looking for them.

Pedro stared at the last hole, down which David and Oji had crawled, half-smiling at the irony of their freedom resting on the shoulders of the African who had become his friend. As the time passed he thought about the night months earlier, when he'd heard from Oji the harrowing story of being a slave taken from West Africa. He'd wept when Oji described the seizing of his family twenty years earlier.

"We were from Benin, five days walking south of the great Niger River, a long way from the Muslims in the north, who had enslaved our people for 800 years."

Pedro had been aghast and embarrassed; Oji's people had lived with the threat of slavery for centuries and less than one year ago he had set out to transport them to the Americas. However, his discomfort got worse.

"We had known about white men coming to Africa for several generations, even my grandfather knew of villages which had been raided by other African tribes, who sold them to the white men at fortresses along the coast, from where they were put onto ships to cross the ocean."

Pedro's heart sank as he listened to a man he'd come to admire.

"Were you not far enough inland to avoid being taken Oji?"

"We were, or at least we thought we were, but as the years passed, stories of our people being seized became more common. The slavers were getting closer, so our elders decided we should move north, further away from the coast and our so-called African brothers who would sell us to your people. Yes, Pedro, I know you are from a country that enslaves Africans, but don't worry my friend, I do not hold you responsible."

Pedro wept but he couldn't tell Oji his story, keeping it to himself through shame.

"I'm sorry Oji, please forgive us."

Oji looked into Pedro's eyes and could guess there was something his friend couldn't say and smiled.

"Despite our fears, your people didn't bring me to Algiers Pedro. We moved further north to avoid the white man's slavery but got too close to the Arabs. Slavers from Songai took my whole family when I was five years old and we became part of the slave route across the Great Desert. We walked for weeks across the sand, stopping at the slave city of Timbuktu, by which time all the old people had died, left where they fell in the sand and rocks for the birds to eat."

The cold factual account Oji gave had sent a chill through Pedro's body and sitting there on the side of the hill, he willed the African to emerge safely.

"In Timbuktu I saw my parents for the last time, as they were sold to a slave merchant in Rabat, whereas I and the other children were sold to a merchant who brought us to Algiers."

Pedro could remember every word of the conversation he had with Oji months earlier, particularly as he described the pain and heartbreak of seeing his mother dragged away by Arabs with hidden faces. Oji explained he had not cried since, even when he was beaten as a child servant by his master in Algiers. After being bought and sold by several masters, as their fortunes rose and fell, he finally ended up in Abdul's bagno, as one of his best oarsmen, then finally the property of Said and Khaled. As he waited with the others, Pedro reflected on the life of Oji, his friend taken captive at the age of five. He vowed that, if they could eventually get to safety and freedom, he would fight for his African friend's feeedom with his life if necessary.

Another hour must have passed and they were beginning to wonder whether the last pair had encountered a problem, or got lost. As the sun moved towards what they knew must be nearly mid-afternoon, like Pedro they were all staring at the hole in the hillside, down which the last pair had disappeared hours ago. Suddenly the black bald skull of the big African appeared and he pulled himself up onto the land, squinting in the bright sunlight. Oji turned, got hold of David's hand and hauled him out of the hole onto the dusty hillside. They stood looking at the other twenty-nine and despite being dirty, bruised and spattered with blood, a broad smile appeared on Oji's face.

"Are you injured, what did you find?" Pedro asked with fading optimism.

For a moment nothing was said and they all feared more disappointment. Then Oji spoke.

"I think God has smiled on us. We found a cave and a boat."

Pedro could have wept tears of joy but managed to compose himself.

"What, you've found a boat. Where, how big, is it being guarded?"

Oji laughed.

"Where? Down there. How big? Big enough. Is it guarded? Well, it was."

"It was? Where are they now? How many of them?"

David answered Pedro's questions.

"There were four of them but we decided to stay and introduce ourselves. That's the blood of three of them on Oji. I managed to take care of the fourth."

The atmosphere of the group changed and the two men were surrounded and thanked. Hugs and kisses from the men and women made it a memorable moment for Oji and David but they weren't safe yet. Calming down they listened to Oji as he told them of the difficulty of crawling through narrow gaps and down dark passageways. He recommended that they make torches from wood and cloth soaked in the oil, which Madeline had packed for cooking purposes. Once that was done, there was no reason to wait and Oji led them down through the hole and into the hillside.

The descent into the hillside was fraught, with almost everyone slipping and suffering bruises at least once. Pedro and Callum were both concerned for Madeline who was older and less confident on the slippery rock, but by insisting she stay close to them and hold their shirts, they were able to support her when she lost her footing. This happened several times but Madeline found herself suspended each time by the strong Portuguese and Englishman.

None of them had done this before and they were surprised by the heat. There seemed to be a lack of air. More than one of them began to think they might be lost and whether they would ever get out of this passage in the bowels of the earth. Eventually they felt a slight change in the air, it was cooler and less oppressive. Pausing to feel it, they realised it came from the sea. The passageway was still dark but as they edged their way forward, the air cooled and they could taste the difference.

"Nearly there!" Oji shouted down the line and there were gasps and some laughter from those at the back.

Finally, as the passageway broadened and the rock below their feet turned to sand, they found themselves walking into light, into a large cave, with the sea just thirty more paces away. Sitting with half of its hull in the water and half on the sand was a vessel that could be described as a large boat but not quite a small ship. It had one mast for a mainsail and a small horizontal bowsprit. It was fifteen to twenty paces in length and each side had five raised oars. Callum and Jack stared at it and looked at each other. Their smiles were instant and the two friends laughed.

"Dear God, perhaps we will make it out of here after all," Jack exclaimed.

His joy was contagious as the group walked over to inspect the vessel. Smiles broke out as they ran their hands along the hull, just as they might stroke a favourite horse or family dog. Spirits were raised and they agreed to rest, eat and sleep before deciding upon their next move but a feeling of optimism covered the group. The Corsairs were highly unlikely to find them that night and the small boat needed some maintenance to make sure it was sea-worthy. Fortunately, their group included more than one craftsman and there were tools in the bottom of the boat.

Callum found himself glancing over at Laura, the only member of the group not smiling or laughing. As he did so she looked up and saw him, almost allowing a slight smile to appear on her lips, but she couldn't. However, he could see in her eyes a glimmer of hope for the first time, and she could see in his fixed eyes and broad smile the affection that had grown in Callum. She wanted to reciprocate but could not, she just returned his stare.

As they settled down for the evening, in Algiers a small galley eased its way into the harbour. Said and Khaled returned a day or two early with a reasonable catch just before the sun started to disappear to the west. They were both pleased with their catch of four Spanish seamen, who had been on a merchant ship heading for France. It seemed to Said that it was not so different to fifteen years earlier when they sailed with Mobasher, except that they did not return with fish but a far more valuable product to sell in the market.

Their good mood lasted only a moment once they had stepped ashore and started to unload their cargo. Khaled saw one of their Corsair guards running to them with an unusually anxious look on his face.

"Khaled, Said, I have terrible news...."

Once the guard had told them of the loss of their property, Said was silent but Khaled flew into a rage, setting about the guard with a small club.

"Stop Khaled, stop. We are going to need all our men, if we are going to find them."

They helped the bloodied guard to his feet and made their way through the streets back to their bagno. It was left to the Corsairs who had gone on the raid to escort the four new captives and the oarsmen back to the bagno. Said and Khaled were anxious to get back to the bagno and the guard was able to explain in more detail what they thought must have happened. Fortunately for him and the other eight Corsairs the blame seemed to rest squarely with the two who were on night duty. What Said could not understand was how the captives could have got the keys from Mehmed if they were locked in the cages? It was only when Khaled asked the guard where Anna was, that they began to suspect what might have happened. Then they learnt that Madeline was gone too.

"Those bitches will pay for this, I swear."

Khaled's rage turned towards the two women as they entered the bagno through the big wooden door.

After surveying the scene inside the room where Mehmed still laid in a pool of his own blood and seeing the bodies of the two guards, Said and Khaled realised this must have been a carefully planned escape. They could not do anything but get it cleared up as it was getting dark and they would need more men. The three corpses were covered in flies so a cart was brought through to the courtyard, onto which they were loaded and covered, ready for burial the next day.

Said lay on his bed trying to sleep but couldn't stop thinking about how this had actually happened? Who devised this plan? Who was their leader? He had to sleep, tomorrow he would get more men and they would recover their property.

Down in the cave, Callum and the others were unaware that when they crossed the cliffs earlier that day, they had been seen by a small shepherd boy who had been sheltering from the midday sun under an olive tree.

Cave

Callum, Jack and Pedro knew they had possibly two nights grace in the cave before a small army of Corsairs would wonder whether they might have escaped to the south of the city and start looking for them there. Thirty-one escaped slaves could hold them off for a while in the narrow passages that led down through the cliffs to the sea, where they sheltered, but not for long. The small ketch had been tended by the two craftsmen in their group, Portuguese Cico and Irish Sean, working tirelessly to customise the vessel which looked unrecognisable. Only fifteen metres in length, with ten oars, which would require twenty men, or women if necessary, the boat didn't resemble anything any of them had seen or rowed in before.

They knew they faced a dilemma that would require a gamble. Stay in the cave and fight facing insurmountable odds of the thirty-one of them against trained and ferocious Corsairs, or make a run for it, sailing out of the cave and into Algiers Bay, where there could be ten to twenty galleys moored. Staying in the cave and killing as many Corsairs as possible before dying had some appeal. But, if they were taken their deaths could be long, if they weren't sold immediately as galley slaves. Callum couldn't bear to think of Laura's fate were she recaptured. They had got this far and they owed it to themselves to continue their escape for as long as possible.

With the ketch alterations now complete, a night-time escape might be their best option, but that risked irreparable damage to the boat if they hit any of the thousand rocks that lined the bay and could only be seen in daylight.

"We will have them coming down that passage sooner rather than later, you know that Callum. Then we will be driven into the sea. They will be upon us as we board the boat and try to make off." Said Jack.

He was not offering a solution but Callum appreciated his honesty, which focused his mind.

"Yes Jack, we need to stay here until it's safe to sail out through the bay. But if, no when, they come we need to hold them off somehow, allowing us time to board and cast-off."

They both sat in silence thinking. Laura brought them some food and water. She could see in their faces they were trying to find a solution to the problem she had also been considering. She stroked Callum's hair and looked at this young man whom she had come to respect, perhaps someone she could even love. She appealed to them to share their thoughts with her, and they explained the predicament, allowing Laura to join the two young men in thought.

"I have an idea." She said suddenly.

Callum and Jack looked at each other.

"Go on Laura, please, share with us."

"Sit down then and I will."

The three of them crouched down, the two young men listening as Laura spoke more words in five minutes than they had heard her utter in four months. Callum was entranced by her beauty but tried to focus on listening, which became easier as her idea was unfurled for them like a beautiful piece of tapestry. They sat listening in silence, and after Laura had finished, they each had a look of astonishment. Jack, as ever the more cheerful, smiled and even Callum could feel optimism for Laura's daring plan.

"Dear God this girl is so beautiful and yet so wise. One of us really should marry her."

Jack's attempt to lift the gloom of their situation was unsuccessful. For a moment Callum almost took the bait his friend laid, yet another tease, but he controlled himself. "You're right" was all he said, passing a glance to Laura that she liked, but still did not allow herself to show. Callum and Jack both wondered if they would ever see her smile, as she started to take control of the situation.

"This isn't the time or place for your fun." Laura's quick reply was made as she got to her feet and as she turned she ordered the two friends, "Follow me. We've got work to do."

They followed her up the passageway, in the direction from which Said and Khaled would come.

Callum, Jack and Laura had been gone ten or fifteen minutes and the others began to wonder what was happening. Oji walked carefully towards the dark and paused, listening for voices. Then out of the darkness they emerged carrying lit torches.

"Sean and Cico, is the boat ready? Could we sail tomorrow?" Callum called.

"Aye Callum, she could sail now and by Jesus with twenty men at these oars, she'll out-run any Barbary galley. I'd swear on it."

Cico just smiled and nodded in support of Sean.

"Well we won't set off tonight in the dark, we might get only five minutes before hitting the rocks and sinking."

Despite his young years Callum had assumed the position of leader and everyone respected him in that role. The serious young man had reinforced that respect when he had volunteered himself to take care of one of the guards back in the bagno.

They all knew this mongrel boat was their best chance of getting clear of Algiers Bay and having a chance of sailing into the open waters of the Mediterranean. After that they could head straight for Spain or France. There was some dispute over where, as some of their band were Spanish, French, Italian, Portuguese, and none of these countries were the preference of those originating from the British Isles. Callum and Jack both preferred the option of heading west, straight through the Straits of Gibraltar, out into the Atlantic and then north for home.

"Well that's a problem we can discuss if we get out of here," said Jack.

Jack, who got on with everyone because of his cheerful nature, got their agreement. Gathered around the small fire, that provided light as the sun went down, Callum explained the plan to everyone. He thought the Corsairs could be close and could come down through the passages from the cliffs any time from tomorrow onwards. Thankfully he was confident they wouldn't try it in the dark, so they could rest for at least one more night.

"We are going to wait until they are almost down here upon us before leaving."

"Why wait for them to arrive Callum, we will be over-run and surely perish." Daniel asked the question with sincerity and respect.

"We want them down here and not up there."

Callum looked up gesturing to the cliffs high above them.

"Up there they could pick us off with arrows, cross-bows and rocks," he explained.

"Sure enough from the clifftop our boat would be an easy target. A large rock thrown from that height would put a hole in the hull that would end any escape," Sean added.

"Jack, Oji, me and two others will hold them off. Don't worry, we have a little surprise for them. When you hear the noise you must all get into the boat and be ready to go. If any of us don't make it to the boat, you go without us. That's an order."

There was a murmur amongst the group, the idea of leaving anyone to the Corsairs was not something any of them wanted to think about.

"At first light we need two of us to swim out to the mouth of the cave to see if there are galleys nearby. Please God there aren't any moored just outside. If we know where they are it will make it easier to choose the right direction when we leave. Changing direction out in the bay would take time which we don't have and the galleys would be upon us."

Everyone began to feel a little more confident after hearing the plan. But they still wondered what the "little surprise" was that could halt the charge of many Corsairs. Jack took over and explained, leaving Callum to collect his thoughts. Once Jack had finished the group looked at one and other, eyebrows were raised and a few smiles appeared.

"I think we have a slave general in Callum." Pedro the Portuguese said with a flashing grin, adding "Let me volunteer to give them their little surprise."

"You're looking at the wrong general Pedro, the plan is Laura's."

"Let me volunteer too." Patrick stepped forward.

"We need to gather all the dry wood there is in the cave and anything else that will burn. We need picks, shovels and the oil too."

At that the five of them and ten others set about collecting dry wood and sailcloth. Fortunately, there was an abundance of it in the cave, most of it washed up during storms. Taking it up the passage into the dark, Callum and Jack directed them in what to do. For three hours they worked by torchlight laying their trap, taking care to not spill any oil which would be applied at the last moment. They returned to the others pleased with their work, although more hopeful than certain that the strategy would work.

That was done, the trap was laid and all they had to do was sit, wait, and try to sleep. Callum lay awake as the fire burnt out and the light faded, then he became conscious of someone moving. Confident it wasn't the Corsairs yet, he thought it was just one of the others disappearing into the shadows to relieve themselves. The footsteps were light across the sand and pebbles, as they came closer he instinctively reached for his sabre. In the shadow of what little light was left he recognised the silhouette as Laura. She bent down, put her finger to his lips and lay closely beside him.

His eyes were wide open as he whispered "What are you doing?"

He could see the white teeth of her smile and smell her body.

"Let me be your woman tonight." Laura kissed him gently but purposefully on the lips. No other words were spoken and for the first time in his life Callum was intimate with a woman. The one he had come to adore.

He was not aware of falling asleep but eventually woke early, as light started to appear through the mouth of the cave. Laura was still there, so close to his face that he could feel her breath and he could have laid there admiring her beauty for hours, letting her sleep peacefully. But he knew he must be alert and carefully extricated himself from her arms and pieces of clothing, getting to his feet as quietly as he could to look at the others sleeping. One person was already awake. Jack had slept far enough away to not hear Laura in the night but had woken early, thinking he would see if Callum was alright. His surprise at seeing them asleep in each other's arms turned to pleasure. In another situation he would have made fun by waking them and enjoying their embarrassment but he was genuinely pleased for his friend, who he had come to love like a brother. 'God knows you deserve at least one night together,' he thought to himself. When Callum saw Jack's huge grin he just put his own finger to his lips and Jack was happy to remain silent.

The two friends went down to check the boat one last time, although what did it matter, if there was a problem it was too late now. Admiring the work of Cico and Sean, they wondered what the small boat would be like with ten oars. If they got out to sea, they would be in charge of sailing and Oji would be in charge of the oars. The coordination of these two sources of power was crucial, if they did not work in unison the boat could capsize. If it was necessary to stop rowing, Jack would shout the instruction to Oji.

Returning to the inner chamber of the cave where they had all slept, they found everyone getting up and gathering their blankets. No-one needed to be told what to do, they got ready without speaking. Before the five made their short way up the passage into the mountain, they all sat down to eat some food and drink some water, more than one of them wondering whether this would be their last meal. There was not much to say, two of the men were swimming out into the bay and back, reporting there were no galleys right outside but they could be seen half a league away. Callum told them to get dry and dressed, there was no point in risking being seen now. Half a league was a decent head start on the Barbary galleys but a good wind would help.

"Remember, when you hear the noise make your way to the boat and get it ready to go. If we're not close behind you, just go."

With that, Callum, Jack, Oji, Patrick and Pedro picked up the oil, as well as some torches and weapons. They took a last look at the others and turned towards the darkness of the passage leading into the mountain. As they left, Callum glanced over to where Laura stood. Her beauty and the intimacy of the last night filled him with determination to make this work. It had to work for her and he would fight to the last to ensure her escape and a chance of freedom. He looked away and followed Jack.

Those who stayed in the cave could see the torches' dim lights, which told them the five were not far and that if the plan did not succeed the Corsairs would be upon them in minutes.

Callum sat the men down at the edge of the place where they would confront the oncoming Corsairs. In truth they didn't know how many they would face but it did not really matter. If the plan worked there could be twenty or two hundred, they didn't care and began to wish the Corsairs would arrive sooner rather than later, so that they could meet their fate. Callum reflected on the last couple of days, Mary's trap for Mehmed, which he and the other men had not known any details of, them sitting and listening to it unfolding, him and Oji taking care of the two guards, Pedro leading them out of Algiers in the darkness, their climb over the clifftops and descent through the passages to the cave. Finally, Laura's idea that could see them halt a unit of skilled fighting Corsairs. He smiled and thought to himself 'We've got this far, surely we can finish it'. If their escape meant that he would fight and perish there in that dark passage, he resolved that was what he would do, ensuring the safety and freedom of Laura and that of the others became his primary motivation.

"We will know when they are approaching as we will see the light from their torches," said Callum. "Then I will line the trap with the oil. Jack will hold the torch, standing back but providing just enough light for me to see what I'm doing. If we're all at the trap and a spark caught the oil we would all burn."

The others listened and nodded.

"If they get through the trap, we will kill as many as possible and hope the others leave in the boat before we fall."

Everyone understood the risk and was ready to die if necessary, giving the others at least a modicum more time.

So they waited in silence, gazing into the darkness, listening for any sound that might give them some idea of numbers. They were left to their thoughts and after some hours it came, a murmur at first, then an echo and eventually the sound of voices speaking Arabic. Because of the narrowness of the passage that wound its way down to sea level, with sharp descents that required clambering, they knew it would take some minutes to reach the trap. The Corsairs were clearly uncomfortable in the mountain descending through the tunnel and passageway, which was borne out by the clattering and cursing as individuals slipped and fell. It was too much to hope they would all fall and break bones but a few did incur injury judging by the howls of pain and calls for help.

Jack sprang to his feet and gestured to the others to drop back ten paces, leaving just him and Callum, both holding a torch. The plan was that they would be the first slaves the Corsairs would see, they would goad them, drawing them into the trap, then retreat hoping the Corsairs would give chase. The passage was not too narrow, allowing a body of men to charge down it maybe ten abreast. This was important and was why this part of the passage had been chosen. It meant that if they were in crowded close quarters up to 200 charging Corsairs could fit into a space just thirty metres in length.

Their torch lights got brighter and suddenly there they were, the bodies if not the faces of the Corsairs could be identified. The tension was unbearable, then a call went up in Arabic and it was clear that they could see Callum and Jack. Said and Khaled stepped forward and their men stopped, standing close behind them. Said called.

"Callum, Jack, there you are, we've been looking for you. Lay down your weapons, join us, we just want our property back. Particularly the girl Laura, she has been promised for the Sultan. He's heard of her beauty and wants her for his harem. You don't want to disappoint the Sultan boys."

Khaled laughed and added.

"If she's been damaged, I'll have her for myself!"

Callum was in no mood to enter into a conversation, he suspected it could be a trick to get them to let down their guard. Rather, he thought he could use the subject of Laura to draw them into the trap. He needed them to come forward fifteen metres and expected them to move quickly when they advanced.

"You're too late Said, they are leaving now, we're here to delay you so you can't get any of them and you won't see Laura ever again Khaled. I hope the Sultan forgives you for failing but I understand he can bear a grudge when he doesn't get what he wants."

They were so close that Callum and Jack could see the rage on Khaled's face, the same look they'd seen before when he was about to slaughter innocent people or kill the enemy.

"Come on, let's take them and get the slaves that belong to us."

Khaled shouted at the men behind him, and with that they bustled forward.

"No Khaled. No!"

Said bellowed, he realised something was wrong but it was too late, Khaled advanced and the men followed. The ground in the dark passage was bumpy with rocks so they couldn't charge and the corsairs were cautious to avoid falling but they moved forward stepping over bits of old tree and sail cloth.

Jack turned and called.

"Man the boat, go now!"

Jack and Callum turned and ran back towards Oji, Patrick and Pedro. As they did Callum held his torch to the left side of the passage and Jack held his to the right, resulting in a line of fire igniting the sides of the passage. The two slaves running and the fire appearing at the sides of the passage caused alarm amongst the Corsairs but they chose not to turn back, giving chase instead. As they entered the prepared space they began to run and this was just as Laura had planned it. They could not see the ground at their feet and the front row of men, including Khaled, crashed to the ground as they trod on a patch of branches that covered a ditch half a man deep. Cries went up as the front row fell and those immediately behind stumbled over them, also falling to the ground. It slowed the whole charge down and at that point all the Corsairs, nearly ninety of them, had crossed the line of bits of wood and sail cloth at the start of the trap. As they did so the fire had spread back behind the Corsairs and a line just behind where Jack and Callum had stood also ignited. The result was that the Corsairs were all crammed into a space thirty metres long, in a passage barely five metres wide and two metres high. The oil-soaked wood and sail cloth produced an inferno in seconds. With the flames and heat having nowhere to escape, it climbed the sides of the passage and swept across the ceiling. The screams of the men were blood curdling but the five men looked on with pride in their work. Standing some way back from the fire they could feel the heat and realised they should get to the boat.

They broke into a trot, making their way down to the cave, where it was a relief to get closer to the cool sea air. All five had singed hair, and were in a mild state of shock at seeing at close quarters the incineration of nearly ninety men. Despite the Corsairs being their enemy they all thought how it must be a terrible way to die. The others were there waiting and the relief on their faces was tangible when they saw it was their men coming and not Corsairs.

"Come on, let's go."

Callum urged everyone onto the boat, which he would be the last to board. As they were almost all on they heard indistinguishable words and turned to see a man with his clothes burnt away and much of his skin too. Most of his hair was gone but Callum recognised Khaled, moving forward holding a large sabre. A man risen from his grave. Callum had put his weapon in the boat and was defenceless as Khaled was upon him raising his sabre for a death blow he had applied a hundred times before. All Callum could do was raise his arms to try to protect his head, as Khaled started to send his sabre through an arc that would cut off any arm and much of his opponents head, he was halted by a blow to his abdomen that came with a piercing pain. Looking down incredulously, Khaled could see that a pike had been thrust through his stomach, with only the wooden pole visible, the metal spike having exited his back. He looked up to see the girl at the other end of the pole. Laura released her hold on the pike, leaned down into the boat and picked up a dagger. Khaled had sunk to his knees, dropped his sabre and held the pike where it entered his body. Laura paused for a moment thinking of how Khaled had molested her, his sweaty body odour, but most of all she thought of his execution of her mother, father and husband in Mevagissey. After months of grieving the pain was still raw. She would not let him see her cry, she walked over to him and stood close.

"Look at me."

Khaled raised his head to look into Laura's eyes, at which point she plunged the blade into his neck, opening a deep wound, from which his blood poured and he slumped to the ground. It was only then as he lay still at her feet that tears fell down her cheeks. The emotions she had denied herself since leaving Mevagissey erupted, causing her body to shake uncontrollably.

Callum stepped forward and gently wrapped his arms around her.

"Come Laura, we must go now." He gently eased her onto the boat, where Mary took her in her arms and twenty oarsmen pushed the boat out towards the mouth of the cave into the bay.

Emerging from the cave Callum was relieved to see the nearest galley was still an eighth of a league away but concerned to see that it was not alone. There were three galleys which were not moored but moving slowly towards them.

"They must be just making their way out of the bay, heading for the open sea. Not what we wanted to see," said Callum to Jack.

Worse was to come. A few minutes later the galleys spotted them and they saw the oars lowered on the three ships. One was large with twenty oars, each powered by four men. Eighty slaves on that one galley, all under the whip, Jack thought to himself. The other two galleys were smaller but still larger than their small boat. Between the three galleys there might be fifty Corsairs, too many to fight and they had no tricks to play in the open sea.

"Oji, we need to row." Jack called to the big African.

Oji led the oarsmen, keeping the strokes co-ordinated, making them as efficient as possible. All the men had all been well trained under the brutal schooling of Taro and Khaled. Now they were rowing uncoerced, rowing for their lives and the little ketch picked up speed. The big problem was the galleys had more oarsmen, they were quicker and began to close in.

"We need the wind." Callum wasn't given to panic but he started to worry. "At this rate they will be upon us before we round the headland."

He looked at Jack and Laura, surely this wasn't the end. Jack called to Oji again.

"Oji, we need more speed, please Oji!"

Oji shouted at the men "Pick it up men!"

He increased the stroke rate and the nineteen men joined him. The result was immediate as the ketch increased its speed. Callum felt some optimism but he knew it would just take the galleys a bit longer to catch them. Sure enough, despite the efforts of the oarsmen, the galleys were now visibly closing in on them.

Callum had turned to the Almighty. "Please God, let the wind blow."

He wanted to unfurl the mainsail but if there was no wind it was just a hindrance and that would slow the boat. They were in the hands of the oarsmen and God. Callum, Jack and Laura were helpless and alternated between urging on the oarsmen and glancing back at the chasing galleys.

The distance between them was down to a tenth of a league and getting less and less. As they reached the headland that marked the northern tip of the Bay of Algiers, Callum and Jack looked at each other and wondered whether it would be better to surrender, as thousands of seamen had done before them. They would be punished but hopefully would live.

"Perhaps some of us would be executed to set an example but most, including the women, would be spared and sold." Jack uttered what they all knew.

"Never! We can't go back. I would rather drown." Laura was insistent and when they considered that their captors would eventually learn of what happened in the cave, they agreed they must out-run the galleys, or die there at sea.

The small ketch turned to the west as they passed the headland and suddenly there it was, a strong wind coming from the East, from where so many slaves were sent.

Callum looked to the heavens "Dear God, thank you."

He quickly moved into action, leaving Jack to steer. He could heave and haul a mainsail as well as any man on the seas, but this one was huge, it might even be too big for a boat of this size. Sean jumped to his assistance.

"Easy with her captain, she's big but needs gentle handling, just like my wife."

Callum laughed as he looked at the Irishman, who could always be relied on to find humour in a situation. Sure enough the mainsail was huge, and as it unfurled and filled with wind, the boat surged forward. The acceleration caused those who were standing to stumble and Laura was almost thrown overboard but managed to hold on. Jack steadied himself at the wheel and let out a cheer.

They had never experienced before the effect of a sharp acceleration on the stroke of the oarsmen, which had been thrown into disorder. Oars clattered and became unsynchronised. The danger was clear to Jack, oars could easily break as they moved individually hitting each other and not moving efficiently as one. He called to Oji to stop, who immediately commanded the oarsmen.

"Raise oars. Raise oars!"

They had done this before, usually when about to board another vessel, but this time they were in an open sea and needed to collect themselves. With the oars out of the sea the boat steadied but was still moving at speed, thanks to the power provided by the wind and the huge mainsail.

Jack let Oji and the oarsmen have a minute to steady themselves, God knows they deserved it, then gave the order.

"When you're ready Oji."

Oji looked up at Jack and nodded.

“Come on men, with me the front four will row, then on my call the next four will follow, then the next four, then the next four, then the last four. We can do this!”

“Ready men, with me the front two oars!”

And the so it began, just the front two oars entered the water together and there was an imperceptible increase in speed.

“Next two oars, follow the two men in front of you, oars in!”

With four oars the speed of the boat increased again.

“That’s good men, next two oars in!”

“Next two oars in!”

“Last two oars in!”

Suddenly the ketch was moving at a speed none of them had ever experienced on land or sea. The controlled rowing of twenty strong synchronised men with the adapted mainsail gave the small ketch so much power that it quickly opened the gap between it and the chasing galleys. After rowing for a short time the galleys began to fade into the distance behind them. The chase was over. They had out-run Barbary galleys and relief and euphoria lifted everyone’s spirits. Oji slowed the stroke to one the men could maintain for hours if necessary.

“Dear God, thank you!” Jack screamed as loud as he could looking up at the blue sky.

Eventually the galleys were completely out of sight, suggesting their captains had given up the chase, choosing to save their oarsmen for another day. Thankfully the Corsairs could not have known what happened in the passage and the cave. The pursuit of the ketch would not have been called off if they had been aware of the fate of the 90 Corsairs.

"We're clear Oji, the wind is enough for now, let the men rest." Jack called.

A broad smile appeared across the face of the beautiful African and he was joined in his pleasure by the rest of the crew. Pedro smiled at his friend, knowing they were clear and that he could at last begin to think about a life he could help him build in Portugal. They had discussed this several times, with Oji saying he did not want to return to Benin.

"Why would I? It's a country where I face the threat of slavery from the white man's African slavers from the south and Arab slavers from the north."

"Oji, come to Portugal with me; it is true my country takes many Africans to our colonies in the Americas, but there are also free Africans living in Lisbon. We can say you're my slave, then have your freedom papers drawn up. You can live alongside us, a neighbour I will protect with my life."

Oji gave it some thought and nodded his agreement. 'Why not', he thought, 'it's as attractive an option as anything I've considered for over twenty years.'

Oji gave the command to the twenty oarsmen. "God is with us, he's answered our prayers at last. Raise your oars men and draw them in."

Jack's grin broadened to a smile and the good-looking young Englishman, who had attracted so many admiring glances back in Devon, began to look like himself once again. Throughout their captivity he had tried to keep his and Callum's spirits positive, but it had been a show. He had not genuinely thought they would ever see home again, not since he was nearly beaten to death by Taro, and having witnessed the execution of Captain Weston, Arthur and Harry. Callum had saved his life that day, which Jack remembered each day since. His hope, rather than belief, that they might survive to see home again was as motivated by a desire to see his friend rewarded, as it was for his own liberty. 'I think we're going to be alright mate', he thought as he caught a glimpse of Callum in the bright sunlight.

With the withdrawal of muscle power the ketch slowed but the strong following wind continued to fill the mainsail, and for the first time all thirty-one of them could relax and begin to think they might finally be free. After an initial euphoria each one of them was left to their own thoughts as a peaceful, calm atmosphere enveloped the small boat. For some, captivity had been a matter of months, for others a year or more, for Madeline it had been decades. Could they really be safely away from Algiers and the bagno? Certainly the way they were able to power away from the galleys gave them confidence in case more possible slavers appeared on the horizon. All of the men were strong and as expert at rowing as any Corsair or Ottoman slave, and they would apply themselves with every muscle and sinew in their bodies.

To make coming across Corsairs less likely, Jack steered them directly west, which they knew would take them straight to the Spanish coastline, as the North African coastline turned gently south-west. This involved just a short crossing across the Mediterranean and they would meet the Spanish coast at a headland, behind which lay the old town of Almeria, from where they could continue sailing west close to land, hopefully safe from recapture. Few Corsairs would risk their own enslavement by sailing so close to Spain, their greatest enemy. Ironic, none of the voyagers on the small boat were to know that passing by Almeria, they were so close to where Said had left Europe twenty-two years earlier.

The quietest person throughout the escape had been Madeline, just as she had been for so many years in the bagno. Like the others the old woman had spent some time looking back towards the south-east, where Algiers lay around the headland, which eventually disappeared from view. Then she turned to face west and north-west, towards where she understood France could be reached. At first she did this with her familiar blank, expressionless look, the mask she had worn for so many years.

Anna moved alongside Madeline, her female companion from the bagno, who had endured the same ordeal but a thousand times more. The younger woman put her arm around Madeline, giving her a gentle squeeze. No words were needed. The old woman felt emotional for the first time in more years than she could remember. Emotions, that she had learnt to confine to a sealed bottle in a corner of her mind, began to reappear. Could she really get back to France? She thought about her children, Cecile and Davide, they had been so young when she last saw them. They would be grown now, possibly with children of their own. Was she being foolish in thinking she could get back to them, after so long of having dismissed the idea as ever being possible and just surviving from day to day? But it was too late, these emotions were out of the bottle, filling her mind, and with that tears streamed down her cheeks. Anna saw something in Madeline's face she had not seen before-hope.

"Madeline, it's going to be alright, don't be afraid."

Madeline's tears continued to flow but with them appeared a smile, something else Anna had never seen before. With one arm around her shoulders, Anna gently pulled the old woman close, kissing her forehead, a tender embrace witnessed by most of the others, who shared the same thought; how much had this woman endured during her time in Algiers.

Only Callum and Jack could not rest completely, continuing to steer and control the sails, but that was not work for them now, it was a pleasure once again, as it had been a few years ago when they first learnt to sail. They took the time to discuss with Pedro where they would go, agreeing to head straight for Gibraltar, which they would pass through slowly at night using just the oars. The twelve men who were from the Iberian Peninsula, France and Italy, as well as Lucia, Paola and Oji, could be landed ashore at a small friendly village which Pedro knew well. From there the remaining seventeen would continue west until they passed the Cape of St Vincent, turn to the north following the Portuguese coastline, across the Bay of Biscay and, with God's will, on to the coastline of either Cornwall or Ireland, whichever one the winds favoured.

Callum kept a close eye on the mainsail but couldn't stop himself from turning around to look at Laura. Her eyes hadn't left him since they'd put to sea but now the tears were gone and she was smiling. The beautiful young woman who had felt nothing but pain and hatred for months walked over to him, folded her arms around his waist, placed her head on his chest and held him tight. Laura thought about everything that had happened, her mother and father, Will, Mevagissey, Algiers. For four months she had resigned herself to a life of misery, in which survival might be best achieved by having no hope, no emotions. Perhaps it was seeing Madeline that made her realise she couldn't give up, she owed it to Mary, John and Will. Now this young man had touched her in a way no-one ever had and she thought last night no-one ever would. Going to him last night was the right thing to do, she knew it was and if he never looked at her again, she had no regret. It did not matter if he loved her, or whether he married her, she felt alive again.

No words were needed, he held her close and looked to the west, as did the other twenty-nine former captives, west towards Gibraltar, the southern tip of Europe and freedom.

Back on the clifftop outside Algiers, a man dragged himself out of the hole that led to the passage into the mountain. His clothes were partly burnt, parts of his arms were darkened and the burns caused him great pain. However, he did not let the pain stop him from climbing up through the shaft he had descended some hours earlier with a company of ninety Corsairs.

Said stood up wincing in the bright sunlight, looked down the shaft, stared out to sea and uttered three words.

"Khaled my brother."

Historical Epilogue

"Britons never, never, never shall be slaves."

The chorus in James Thomson's Rule Britannia written in 1740, became an anthem for British pride and identity. However, as Laura Baddow, Callum Longbow and the other characters in this story found, it was far from the reality for thousands of Britons and Irish, along with hundreds of thousands of other Christian Europeans, in the sixteenth, seventeenth and eighteenth centuries.

After 1631, the year of this story, raids by Barbary Corsairs continued. The cities of Algiers, Tunis and Salle in Morocco were the main centres, from which the slavers operated. Between 1580 and 1680, Algiers, the largest, held and traded on average 25,000 slaves each year, the total for all of the Barbary Coast being on average 35,000 each year for the same period. The Ottoman Empire had on average 300,000 slaves in chains each year for the period 1500 to 1800. Istanbul, the centre of the empire is estimated to have had 100,000 slaves in 1609, one fifth of the city's population.

Even though the forty years between 1610 and 1650 may have been the nadir for the seizing of British and Irish captives, through the seventeenth century the situation did not improve a great deal. Barbary slavers from Algiers captured 353 ships from the British Isles between 1672 and 1682, which would have resulted in slavery or death for their crews. This was despite the creation of the Royal Navy in 1660, with the restoration of Charles II.

The development of an English and later British navy was important. Early in the sixteenth century when Henry VII died in 1509, he left his seventeen year-old son and heir, Henry VIII, a navy comprising of just three ships. When Henry VIII died in 1546, he left his young son, Edward VI, a total of fifty-eight vessels of different sizes. Henry VIII had been able to finance his navy from the windfall of looted monastic wealth. His daughter, Elizabeth I, saw the navy as critical in the defence of the nation from the Spanish, which resulted in a fleet of 110 ships against the Armada in 1588. However, over the first sixty years of the seventeenth century the navy became primarily concerned with fighting the French, the Dutch, the Spanish and developing a stronghold in the 'New World'. It was not used to protect English, Irish or Welsh shipping from North African slavers.

For the purposes explained above, the navy was expanded, largely by the Republican English Parliament in the 1650s. In 1642, Parliament took control of a fleet of just thirty-five ships, which by 1660 and the beginning of Charles II's reign, numbered 157 ships and more than 21,000 men. This growth in the navy coincided with a decline in Britons and Irish captives but it was not causal.

In 1677 the navy was sent to Algiers in a war that lasted until 1682 and was costly, both financially (over £800,000) and over 160 ships destroyed, as well as in human terms with over 3,000 taken captive as slaves. At the end of this conflict a treaty was signed with Algiers and shipping from the British Isles was safe from Algiers Corsairs, brought about through diplomacy. Unfortunately, along the coast from Algiers another state emerged as a major threat to Christians at sea. Morocco, which had resisted control from the Ottoman Empire, came under the rule of Sultan Moulay Ismail in 1672, until his death at the age of eighty-one in 1727. All captives taken by Morocco's corsairs became his personal property, slavery becoming a state organised business.

Sultan Moulay Ismail was less interested in selling captives to the Ottoman Empire than Algiers. He used them for hard-labour, for building harbour walls, fortifications, palaces and the development of towns. However, he became very skilled at seizing captives and ransoming them back to their countries of origin. In 1721, a British mission sent to Morocco to recover over 300 captives, paid for them with over 1,200 barrels of gunpowder and 13,500 gun-locks. Morocco became stronger and Moulay Ismail's army was estimated at 150,000, compared to 30,000 in the British Army.

This lack of effective military success against the Barbary Coast slavers was not confined to Britain. In 1775, at a time when Britain was increasingly occupied in America and India, Algiers repelled an attempted Spanish invasion of 300 ships and 22,000 men.

In 1756 Parliament sent a particularly inept Captain Hyde to Morocco, to negotiate a treaty and the release of British captives. Hyde's rudeness and lack of respect to the future Sultan, Sidi Muhammed, caused a major incident and breakdown in British-Moroccan relations. The result was that within two years Morocco had taken another 400 captives, William Pitt the Elder had to apologise to Morocco and Britain paid 200,000 Spanish dollars for their release.

It should be remembered that slavery in the Mediterranean and European seaboard region was not solely one-way, with only Muslim slavers from North Africa seizing white Christians. In 1673 it was reported that 2,000 Muslims rowed on French galleys. In Naples 400 Muslim slaves worked from 1753 to the end of the century on the royal palace at Caserta. However, most of white Europe's slave enterprise had moved to Africa and the Americas.

Finally, not until the end of the eighteenth century and the defeat of the French in the Napoleonic War did the situation change dramatically for seamen and travellers from the British Isles. By the end of that war in 1815, the British Navy finally *ruled the waves* and Britons would *never be slaves.*

Bibliography

L Colley Captives, Britain, Empire and the World 1600-1850, Pimlico, 2003

R C Davis Christian Slaves, Muslim Masters, Pelgrave McMillan, 2003

B Hughes Istanbul, A Tale of Three Cities, Weidenfeld and Nicholson, 2017

B Lavery Empire of the Seas, Bloomsbury, 2015

P Mansell Constantinople, City of the World's Desire, John Murray, 1995

O'Connell and Dursteler The Mediterranean World: From the fall of Rome to the rise of Napoleon, John Hopkins, 2016

D J Vitkus Piracy, Slavery, and Redemption: Barbary Captivity Narratives from Early Modern England, Columbia, 2001

B Wilson Empire of the Deep, the Rise and Fall of the British Navy, Weidenfeld and Nicholson, 2013